Kisses For Sale

Judith Enderle

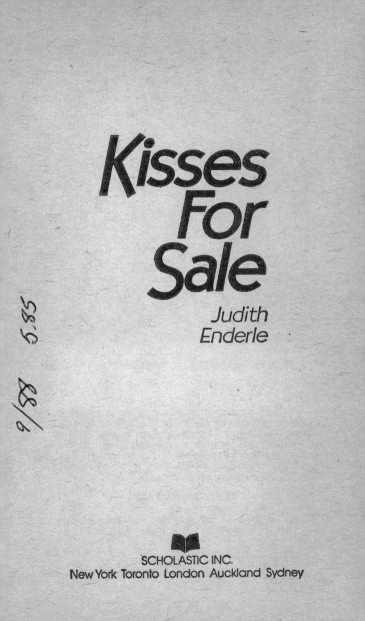

SCHOLASTIC INC.
New York Toronto London Auckland Sydney

For Monica and Jackee, independent women

ISBN 0-590-33262-7

12 11 10 9 8 7 6 5 4 3 2 1   7   5 6 7 8 9/8 0/9

Printed in the U.S.A.   06

Kisses For Sale

A Wildfire Book

WILDFIRE® TITLES FROM SCHOLASTIC

One

When the boy who promised he'll love you forever doesn't love the real you anymore, what do you do?

Hairbrush in hand, Lindsey stretched across her lavender spread and let her head droop over the edge of the bed. "You don't sit around and cry forever," she said through gritted teeth. "You get busy and you stay busy." Vigorously she yanked the brush through her shoulder-length dark blonde hair and tried to ignore the puffy, burning sensation behind her eyes. "Stupid to cry," she muttered.

Nine whole days had passed since she and Ross had shouted ultimatums at each other, then broken up. Everything reminded her of him, even the telephone sitting silent on the table beside her bed. Ross used to call every evening.

"Are you talking to yourself again, Lin?" Her twelve-year-old sister Trina twirled through the doorway and sat on the carpet beside the bed. "Ross isn't worth all the tears you're wasting over him, you know." She spoke matter-of-factly.

Lindsey sat up and pushed her hair over her shoulders. "Were you spying and eavesdropping again, Trina?" The snap in her voice made her sound witchy. Quickly she wiped a hand across her eyes, catching a couple of tears before they were too noticeable. She sighed. "Sorry, Trina. I didn't mean to yell at you." She continued to brush her hair — softer, pensive strokes now.

Trina shrugged and tied her long braids in a loop under her chin. "I could have told you, Lin." Her wide blue eyes, identical to Lindsey's, looked all-knowing. "Ross couldn't be trusted. Look how he always treated me; a piece of dirt got more notice. Of course you *know* how he hated to get dirty.

"Remember when Piper was a brand new puppy and he fell asleep on Ross's jacket? You'd have thought our poor baby basset hound did something much worse, the way Ross yelled." Trina giggled, then grew immediately sober. "Piper never liked Ross after that. He always remembered."

"Enough, Trina!" Lindsey knew she sounded angry again. "Anyway, trust had nothing to do with our breaking up," she added.

"Well, I don't know exactly what happened, but I think trust had everything to do with it. If a boy says he loves you for almost a whole year, then he doesn't, I wouldn't call that trustworthy."

"Trina . . ."

Her sister popped to her feet. "All right! I won't say any more about him. But if you want to talk later, let me know. That's what sisters are for." She danced out the door and called, "Piper. Here, Piper. Time for you to go outside."

Obviously not everyone felt bad about Ross and Lindsey breaking up. But Lindsey felt at loose ends and a bit scared. Being in Ross's shadow had held a kind of security, even if it had been an isolated kind. With Ross, there hadn't been room for many close friends. At least Blaine had kept in touch. Lindsey was going to need her best friend a lot now.

Fighting sluggishness, she forced herself to get up from the bed. But indecision followed her, and she stood in the center of her room wondering how she could possibly stay busy enough to keep Ross out of her thoughts.

"Being in his shadow seems to be enough for Ruthanne Kramer," she muttered, shaking off depressing memories. Ruthanne had been seen often with Ross during the past week.

Lindsey wished she could rid herself of the doubts that continued to assail her. She felt like a stretched rubber band and just as vulnerable to flying off in any direction. One minute she felt determined and confident that breaking up with Ross had been the right thing to do; the next, she worried that she'd made a mistake.

After opening her closet to choose what she'd wear to school in the morning, she resisted the urge to take down the photograph of Ross that was hidden between the shoe boxes on her shelf. "I have to get used to being me again," she muttered. "That's what I wanted." She pulled her turquoise jeans and checkered shirt from their hangers, then quickly closed the closet door. That's what the argument had been about: being independent, being her separate self — something Ross couldn't handle. Lindsey wondered if any boy could.

When she went to the window to pull the shade against the darkness, she caught a glimpse of her solitary figure in the glass. "I *did* make the right choice," she whispered. But what price equality? What price independence? she wondered.

Once again forcing herself into action, she headed for the shower. Tomorrow would start day number ten. She'd made it through another weekend.

At least the nights went fast. The alarm clock buzzed beside her, and Lindsey haphazardly patted the table, trying to silence its nagging noise. She touched the snooze button for three more minutes of blessed silence and rolled over. But the alarm had done its job.

The cinnamon scent of raisin-bread toast and the rich aroma of fresh coffee floated up from the kitchen. Lindsey got up and went through her routine preparations for school.

"See you later. Have a good day at school." Her father hugged her on his way out the door to his district manager's job at Friendly's Fine Foods.

"Yes, Mom, I have my books. Yes, I did my homework. Yes, I have my lunch money. No, I won't be late. Yes, I'm feeling fine." Lindsey sat at the table in the cheerful yellow and white kitchen and answered the litany of questions before they were asked.

Her mother had added the latter question last week. Lindsey knew what she was asking about, but she didn't want to talk about Ross with her parents. Trina was the only family member who'd heard any of the details of the break-up. And that was because she was as persistent as a gnat, buzzing in and out of Lindsey's room with a question here, a comment that required a response — like last night. Lindsey guessed that her sister kept their parents informed.

She ate a slice of toast and drank a glass of milk quickly.

"It's a beautiful morning," her mother said. "Every cold Michigan winter is worth it when spring arrives. You won't need more than a light jacket today." Her voice sounded overly cheerful.

Lindsey glanced at her mother's face and noted the concern there. Frown lines etched her forehead, and strands of gray threaded through her light brown curls. Lindsey tried to smile reassuringly, before she gathered her books, gave Piper a good-bye pat, and left the house.

Her friend Blaine was already on the bus, saving a seat. "Isn't it a super morning? I have an astronomical case of spring fever. The forsythia bush by our back door looks like sunshine in bloom. And there's a robin building a nest in our porch light. You'll have to come and watch. The lilacs are just starting to bud. My mother says they have the scent of heaven and . . . Lindsey, you haven't heard a word I've said." Blaine touched Lindsey's shoulder.

"Everyone's talking about spring." Lindsey stared out the window at the brown lawns and trees that only hinted at awakening to warmer weather. Forsythia, the way Blaine had described it, was like a beacon of brightness in several of the yards they passed. They swayed in their seats as the bus rode through the curving streets of the subdivision, then bumped out onto the main road and turned toward the next stop.

"Can you blame them? After this winter, most people had doubts we'd ever see a warm day again. Besides, the weather is a nice neutral topic. Would you rather talk about Ross?"

Lindsey looked at her friend. "No! Yes! I don't know," she finished with a sigh.

Blaine nodded knowingly. Her permed

curls sprang softly around her slightly plump face. "Want some advice?"

"You'll give it to me anyway."

"But will you listen?"

"Sure. What's your advice, Mother Blaine?"

"Get involved in something to keep your mind off Ross."

"Such as? Everything reminds me of him, even when I don't want it to. I'm trying to keep busy, Blaine. Bet I've done more studying and reading these past nine days than I'd done since I started high school."

"Don't exaggerate, Lin."

"I'm not. Really. Blaine, sometimes I wonder if I didn't overdo my independence speech. I mean, before I had a boyfriend. Now what do I have?"

"Your self-respect," said Blaine, who was the only one who knew every detail of what had happened between Lindsey and Ross. "And there will be other guys — guys who don't need a girl to be an extension of their egos."

"Hah! I'm not so sure. Can a girl be independent and have a boyfriend, too?"

"If any girl can, you can. Ross wasn't right for you. I could have told you that a long time ago."

"Now you sound like Trina."

"Your little sister has a lot of smarts, just like you."

"If I'm so smart, why do I feel so miserable?"

"Withdrawal. You had no idea how dependent you'd become on Ross. What else did you have? Ladies who waited went out with knights in shining armor. Girls are people, too. Did he encourage you to run for a class office? Did he encourage you to try out for the pep squad or the softball team? Did he even encourage you to be a library aide? Of course not. He needed you to adore him. *You* were Ross Jordani's decoration." Blaine folded her arms and looked fierce.

"Come on, Blaine. Aren't *you* exaggerating now?"

"Am I?"

Lindsey shrugged and sighed aloud.

The bus rumbled to a halt. Half a dozen more Woodcreek High students paraded on. Next stop was school. "Now is your chance to try something you've always wanted to try," Blaine said, relaxing again.

"Back to that old question: such as?"

"Such as Spring Carnival. The Service Club has to top the funds raised last year — that's tradition. Each year we've done better, but we need a lot of help. Every student is automatically a Service Club member. That was one organization Ross couldn't keep you from joining. But now you can be an *active* member. It's not too late to sign up for the carnival planning committee. How about it?"

Lindsey barely heard her friend's last words. Memories of last year's Spring Carnival and the fun she had there with Ross assaulted her. She pushed them out of her mind. Blaine was saying the same thing she'd been telling herself: She had to keep busy to blot out the past. "All right. Put my name on the top of your volunteer list. I'll be so busy, I won't have time to think."

Blaine bounced in the seat and smiled. "Super! First meeting is after school today. And remember, no backing out."

Lindsey ducked a paper wad that came flying from the back of the bus. The closer they got to school, the noisier the students got. "I said I'd help and I will," she shouted. "Why would I back out?"

Blaine seemed suddenly distracted as she turned to look behind them.

Her friend's intense interest in the other bus riders, whom they saw almost daily, made Lindsey suspicious. An uncomfortable thought occurred to her. She tugged on her friend's sleeve. "Ross didn't decide to be on the committee, did he? Or Ruthanne?"

Blaine's laughter answered both questions. "You must be joking." Her brown eyes sparkled as she turned back to look at Lindsey; her smile was so wide that dimples dotted both cheeks.

Lindsey had the instant impression of her friend mounted on springs and ready to pop sky-high any minute. "I've seen that look before, Blaine. You're up to something. I want to know what before we get to school. You have exactly two minutes to tell me why you look the way you do."

As if to share intimate secrets, Blaine leaned close. "It all has to do with my parents, Lin. You see, my father and mother both have brown hair and brown eyes, so when I was born — " she began with mock seriousness.

"Blaine Harris!"

"Well, I'm not adopted. I'm sure that's the only explanation for my super good looks." Blaine grinned.

Lindsey refused to smile back. She stared at her friend.

Blaine sighed. "All right. Bill Stark is head of the carnival committee this year."

"Oh no! Not the Bill Stark who went to junior high with us? He was never serious. We won't get a thing planned."

"You promised you wouldn't back out." Blaine pulled her book bag from the floor as the bus jerked to a stop in front of Woodcreek High. The doors banged open.

Lindsey edged into the chaos in the aisle and let Blaine step in front of her. Their conversation was temporarily interrupted as they were carried to the door and out onto the walk by the press of disembarking students.

"Anyway," said Blaine, as they strolled up the steps to school, "you don't know the real Bill Stark. He's changed since junior high. You've been too wrapped up in Ross to notice anyone else." It was obvious from her tone of voice that she wasn't teasing now. She reached for the door as the student in front of them let go, holding it until the next hand grabbed it.

Typical of the beginning of the week, the school halls smelled of floor wax. The shine, however, which had been applied over the weekend, was already fading under the soles of several hundred tennis and other assorted shoes. "I don't want to notice anyone else," said Lindsey, as they reached their lockers, which were across from each other. "I'm done with bowing and scraping," she continued, as she twisted the combination dial on her locker. "Boys don't want girlfriends, they want slaves. I won't tolerate chauvinism. I'm now an independent woman." She ignored the kids passing by who turned to look at her as she recited her speech.

Blaine bumped her locker door closed with her hip. She came to wait beside Lindsey. "Not all boys are alike. And you're confusing independent with alone, Lin. You've always been independent — sort of. Now you're alone — or at least you're without a boyfriend."

"Be honest, Blaine. I wasn't all that independent. Certainly not independent enough." Lindsey sighed. Her need for that very thing had driven her and Ross apart. If only he'd been willing to give her a little room, a little breathing space, time to be herself.

"You're hurting. You can't judge all boys by Ross, who — and you needn't pardon me for saying so — is a prime example of a chauvinist. He's what my mother calls overbearing and a few other not-so-complimentary words." Blaine peered into the tiny mirror on Lindsey's locker door. "I need a complete overhaul. Let's stop in the girls' bathroom."

Lindsey slammed her locker door and resisted the urge to defend Ross. Old habits were hard to break. "Come on. I need a pit stop, too," she said.

They squeezed into the crowded girls' bathroom. Talk of weekend dates, the upcoming rock concert, papers due this week, echoed around them

Blaine held their books while Lindsey stepped into the first empty stall. After washing her hands, Lindsey pulled a comb through her hair. Then it was her turn to take the stack of books. "You sounded like a promoter for Bill Stark. Any special reason?" she asked.

Blaine looked surprised. She snapped the top back on her lipstick tube. "Uh-uh. Now Ryan O'Connor is another story. I almost asked him to eat lunch with me last week." For a second, she had a dreamy look in her eyes, but the sound of the warning bell snapped her out of it.

"Almost asked Ryan?" Lindsey repeated.

"Yeah. Ryan," she said. "He's new in school, but you probably didn't notice him, either. Anyway, I lost my nerve and didn't ask." She eased her books from the bottom of the pile.

"What about Bill?" Lindsey asked.

"Bill? Oh, Bill. He's just a nice guy, that's all."

Back in the hallway, they pressed against the wall. Grand Central Station at rush hour had nothing on the between-class rush at Woodcreek.

"I'm qualifying my offer to be on the carnival committee," said Lindsey.

"You promised," Blaine said, getting her stubborn look.

"I didn't say I wouldn't. I will, providing you promise not to push any boys at me or to push me at any boys. Deal?"

Blaine shook her head. "Honestly, Lindsey. Don't you trust your best friend?"

"Promise," said Lindsey, as the second bell shrilled overhead.

Blaine put a hand over one ear. "I can't hear you," she shouted. "Meet me by my locker after school." Then she was gone, one of the crowd of students headed to first period class.

Lindsey let herself blend with the flow, too. She forced her attention away from the faces of the students who passed. In her effort not to look for Ross, she found herself wondering instead about Bill Stark. He's a senior this year, she thought with surprise. Having been out of circulation, she hadn't noticed Bill lately, but the boy she remembered was small and thin with unruly brown hair and mischievous green eyes. And in junior high, everyone — even the teachers — had called him Stark the Spark.

Two

Lindsey's stomach churned nervously as she followed Blaine into the home economics room where the Service Club held its meetings. The faint smell of peanut butter cookies, today's lesson, lingered in the air. She hadn't felt like a new kid on the block in a long time. Had she made a mistake agreeing to help?

She glanced at the others who were waiting for the meeting to begin. She knew Monica, John, and Alicia, who were huddled in a private conversation.

"There's Ryan." Blaine nodded toward a stocky, medium-height boy with sandy hair and a smattering of freckles across his broad nose. He was drawing a cartoon duck on the chalkboard.

That means the other boy is Bill, Lindsey thought with surprise. How could she have missed noticing him? His hair was still brown and curly. But small, thin Bill Stark was now six-foot, muscular Bill Stark.

"Glad you could make it, Blaine," Bill said, as they approached the circle of desks he was pushing into place. His voice was deep and sounded sincere.

His eyes were the same green Lindsey had remembered, but she wasn't sure it was mischief she saw reflected in them now, as his gaze intercepted hers. She looked away first but casually, trying to hide the slight embarrassment at being caught staring.

"You know Lindsey Warren, don't you, Bill?" Blaine asked.

He frowned. "You went to Farmington Meadows Junior High?"

Lindsey nodded. "I remember you, Stark the Spark."

He laughed. "Glad to have the chance to get acquainted or I guess I should say reacquainted." He sounded uncertain.

Lindsey was surprised at the irritation she felt at his lack of recognition. She'd been student council rep in seventh grade, the same year he was rep for the eighth grade. Oh, well, she thought, what did it matter now? She was here to work, to keep busy.

"Is anyone else coming?" Alicia asked. She was tall with dark eyes that looked beautiful behind her pink-tinted glasses with the faceted lenses.

"I guess not," John said. "Let's get started. Today was last call for the planning committee." He lounged in the desk beside Monica.

His long legs stretched into the center of the circle. He let one arm hang casually over the back of the chair. "Looks as if we're it."

"We should start by nominating an official chairman," Monica said

"Chairperson," Lindsey said.

"Someone in charge." John picked up on her comment. "Bill, since Mr. Harley appointed you to organize us, you run the meeting again for now."

"All right. Service Club Carnival Planning Committee meeting is now called to order. Before we get to business, has everyone met Lindsey?" Bill asked.

They all nodded. Her smile felt pasted on.

"I want to make the first motion," Blaine said. "I move that we have two chairmen — chair*persons*," she corrected. "Lindsey and Bill."

"Seconded," Alicia said immediately. "Thank goodness you didn't nominate me. I'm really pressed for time."

"You still have to come to the meetings," Ryan said. "But I'm in favor of the nomination and second it, too, or am I supposed to third it? I never can remember the rules."

"Isn't he darling?" Blaine whispered behind her hand.

"Never mind him. Why did you nominate me?" Lindsey returned. She didn't feel ready to head a committee. And she thought all this had already been decided. Hadn't Blaine said that Bill headed the committee? It certainly seemed as if he did. If the principal,

Mr. Harley, had appointed him, that's the way it should be, she thought.

"To keep you busy." Blaine winked. "Don't worry. You can do it."

"Blaine, I. . . ."

Her friend turned toward Alicia, cutting off any further discussion.

"Oh, I'll be here and do my part," Alicia was saying, while she cleaned her glasses on the sleeve of her sweat shirt. "I just don't want to be in charge of the entire carnival."

"All in favor of Lindsey and Bill," John said.

Five ayes signaled unanimous agreement.

"I guess that means we're co-chairmen," said Bill, glancing at Lindsey.

"Co-chairpeople," she said.

"Whatever the title, you'll do equal work." He looked amused. "Would you like to review what we've done in the past, Lindsey?" He held up a thick notebook.

"You go ahead, Bill, since you're obviously prepared." She glanced at Blaine, who looked as if she'd won first prize in something.

Briefly Bill went over the previous year's budget and the carnival features. "We can do much better, I know," he said, closing the notebook.

"That's agreed upon." Monica wrapped a blonde curl around her finger. She frowned. "But to do that, we need some new attractions. Pitching softballs or trying to break balloons is getting boring — although I suppose we'll keep those for the people who love them."

"I agree. We need some new, old-fashioned attractions. That's the atmosphere we want to maintain — old-fashioned. How about a beauty contest and a kissing booth?" Bill asked.

"You can't be serious," said Lindsey.

"You don't like my suggestions, co-chairperson?" he asked.

Lindsey forgot about being unknown and uncomfortable. "Kissing booths and beauty contests are sexist ideas. Bill, John, Ryan, are you guys going to parade around in shorts or bathing suits to be judged? Are you going to sell kisses?"

"I look pretty good in a bathing suit," Bill said.

The others laughed.

"And what would you offer for a kiss from Stark the Spark?" He leaned close to Lindsey.

"Nothing," she said coolly. He wouldn't get a spark out of her.

"Then you can see why I wouldn't be selling kisses." His eyes seemed to twinkle.

Obviously he isn't one bit serious, Lindsey thought.

"Everyone, Lindsey is right," said Blaine. "Your suggestions are *too* old-fashioned, Bill, and sexist."

"Lindsey does have a valid point. How about a congeniality contest instead of a beauty contest?" Monica suggested. "Everyone would be eligible for that."

"Not visual enough." Ryan stretched his arms and cracked his knuckles. "How about a beauty contest for dogs?"

"Great idea!" Lindsey said, thinking about Piper, who was the most beautiful basset hound she knew.

"Does *everyone* agree?" Bill looked directly at Lindsey.

"Not everyone has a dog," John said. "How about all pets?"

"Oh, yes!" Blaine said enthusiastically. "And anyone who doesn't have a pet could choose a pet for that day," she continued. "Pet worms, pet crickets, pet teddy bears. Whatever an entrant wants to count as a pet, counts."

"Perfect solution." Ryan nodded.

"Monica, pet," said John with an exaggerated wink.

Monica wrinkled her nose at him, while Lindsey shook her head. He wasn't any more serious than Bill.

"Does everyone agree that the pet beauty contest is a good idea?" Bill asked.

Now everyone did.

He wrote in the notebook. "Now, about the kissing booth," Bill continued, obviously not willing to give up both his old-fashioned ideas. "If it's all in good fun and staffed by both boys and girls, I think it would be a good money-maker. What do you think?" Again he looked at Lindsey.

"You'd have to pay your money before you got a kiss," said Alicia.

"Well, I'm not going to kiss Bill, not even for free," Ryan teased.

"Don't worry. We'll fix you up with Blaine," John said.

Both Blaine and Ryan blushed.

"I still don't think —" Lindsey began.

"You take charge of the kissing booth, Lindsey," Bill suggested. "I'm sure you can work out a fair and equal system."

"Good idea," Alicia said. "And pray there isn't a mono epidemic this spring."

"Don't let Mr. Harley hear you say that," John said. "Our beloved principal has ultimate veto power over all our ideas."

"Well, I think that's another reason . . ." Lindsey began.

"You can do it, Lin," Blaine said. "Take charge of the kissing booth."

"What do you say, Lindsey?" Bill's eyes seemed to challenge her. He held his pen poised over the notebook page.

"I didn't volunteer to take charge of the kissing booth," she said. "I still don't agree that it's a good idea."

"You don't think you can do it?" Bill asked, putting the pen down.

"I didn't say that."

"Then you will?"

"We gave in on the old-fashioned beauty contest," John said. "And I was even planning to be the judge."

Lindsey glared at him.

"Does anyone else want the job of running

the kissing booth?" Bill asked, though he still looked at her.

They all looked at her. No one volunteered.

Lindsey sighed with exasperation. They were trying to goad her into agreement. "All right. I'll be in charge of the kissing booth." She glared at Bill, then at Blaine. She'd show them how a kissing booth should be run. They'd be surprised.

"Moving right along," Bill said smoothly after making another note, "Alicia, will you take charge of the crafts booths?"

"Can't I do the shows?" she asked.

"I'll take the crafts," Ryan said.

"I'll take the games," Monica said.

"Shows for you then, Alicia." Bill wrote rapidly.

"Let me handle the beauty contest," said John. "If I can't be a judge of a real one, I can at least appreciate the animals."

"It's all yours," Bill said. "I'll contact the company about renting the kiddie merry-go-round. That was a money-maker last year. Blaine, will you get some volunteers to be in charge of food?"

"I volunteer," said Ryan.

"Do you want to do both crafts and food?" asked Bill.

"Sure. I'll help Blaine and she can help me."

Blaine nodded and smiled with obvious agreement and pleasure.

Decorations, the construction schedule for

the booths, advertising, and other details were assigned to Lindsey and Bill, traditional responsibilities of co-chairpeople. A weekend date was chosen as the perfect time to hold the carnival.

Lindsey looked at Bill. Some co-chairperson he is, she thought. He stuck me with the kissing booth, but hasn't offered to do anything extra except rent the merry-go-round. Well, Blaine was right about one thing: He can be serious and take charge, Lindsey mused. But he's too darned bossy and sure of himself.

"What do you think, Lindsey?" Bill asked.

She was startled from her thoughts. "About what?"

"You must have been dreaming up some special kisses," he teased.

"You'll find out soon enough." She refused to let him upset her.

John whistled softly under his breath.

"She didn't mean what you're thinking, John Tyler." Monica poked him.

"I asked about a competition to see which booth or show brings in the most funds," Bill said.

"I've changed my mind again," said Ryan. "I'll do shows. How about belly dancing?"

John clapped.

"Some helper you are, Ryan O'Connor. If you quit on me, I'll quit on you." Blaine was obviously trying to keep her voice light, but Lindsey knew she was upset. Her friend probably had read more into Ryan's offer to help then he'd meant.

"If you have the belly for it, go to it, Ryan," said Alicia.

"Beware of Alicia, insult expert," Ryan said. "I was kidding."

"I thought you were dancing," Bill said. "Dah-dah dah doh dah. Dah-dah dah-dah dah-dah dah," he sang.

Lindsey closed her eyes and shook her head. This kind of banter wouldn't have bothered her before her break-up with Ross. She probably wouldn't even have noticed what was being said. Am I being oversensitive? she wondered.

She felt a hand on her shoulder. She thought it was Blaine, but was surprised to open her eyes and find that it was Bill.

"Belly dancing won't ever get approval from Mr. Harley," he said. "Let's get this meeting back to order."

"If girls belly dance, boys belly dance," said Lindsey, jumping into the discussion.

"Well, you haven't seen my act." John tried to stand up, but Alicia and Monica pulled him back down.

"They don't want to see," Monica said.

Bill tapped his pen on the desk. "What about some booth competition, everyone?"

"The food booth with chocolate chip cookies and brownies will win," said Blaine. "It always brings in the most money. There's no competition."

"Then you want to veto that idea?" Bill asked.

"Vetoed," John said. The rest agreed.

"Then I'm back on the food committee," Ryan said.

"Just watch you don't eat all the profits," Blaine teased, sounding happy again. "Lindsey, will your dad help us with the food?"

"I'm sure he will. I'll ask."

"Her dad's district manager of Friendly's," Blaine explained.

"Good." Bill made a note. "Now let me throw out a few more ideas: a dunk tank, a pie-throwing booth, a spaghetti-eating contest."

"Stop," Ryan groaned. "I'm starving."

"Me, too," said Blaine. "Can't we call this meeting to a close? Next time let's meet at Frannie's Pantry."

"I'll second that," Alicia said.

"I move that we adjourn the meeting," said Lindsey, taking the cue, "but I say yes to Bill's last ideas."

Blaine seconded the motion.

"Moved and seconded. Meeting adjourned. Next meeting a week from today. We'll discuss those last few ideas then. Have some definite plans for your areas." Bill tapped Lindsey's arm and pushed a slip of paper in front of her. "Would you write your phone number?" he asked.

"My phone number?" she repeated.

"Co-chairpeople have to get together to do further planning sometimes. I might call you later."

She looked away from his green eyes. Was he teasing her again? she wondered.

"Sure." She jotted her number and handed the paper back to him.

"Talk to you later." He smiled and tucked the paper in his shirt pocket. He picked up his books. "Does anyone need a ride home?"

"I do." Alicia swung her book bag onto her shoulder.

"So do we," Blaine said.

Lindsey poked her in the back.

"Come on. I have the station wagon," Bill said. "I'll play taxi for all of you."

"We could have taken the bus," Lindsey muttered to Blaine as they trailed after the others.

"And miss out on the chance to ride with Ryan?"

Lindsey felt guilty. She'd been so busy thinking about herself being thrown together with Bill that she'd forgotten Blaine liked Ryan.

Lindsey slid into the back seat with Blaine and gave directions to her house. When the car stopped in front of the neat brick colonial where she lived, she hopped out quickly.

Bill rolled the car window down. "I'll call you later," he said.

What could she say? What would they have to talk about? "Thanks for the ride," she said.

"I'll call you, too," Blaine called.

When Lindsey opened the front door, she caught Trina with her nose pressed to the living room window.

"Who brought you home?" Trina didn't even look around.

"Bill Stark. We're heads of the committee for Spring Carnival."

"You are? Will you get free tickets? Can I go?" Trina let the curtain fall back in place. "Can I invite my friends? Is Bill nice?"

"Stop the questions."

"But I want to know," said Trina. "Was he the one driving or the one in back beside Blaine?"

"I won't get free tickets. You can go if you buy a ticket and the same goes for your friends. And he was the one driving."

"You didn't answer one of my questions."

"What was it?" Lindsey avoided her sister's glance. She went into the kitchen and took an apple from the basket on the counter.

"Is Bill nice?"

"He's okay," Lindsey said through a mouthful of apple. A little too sure of himself, she thought. She glanced toward the phone.

As she climbed the stairs to her room, Lindsey realized that she'd hardly thought about Ross at all that day. Keeping busy was the answer. But not with a kissing booth. What kind of kissing booth could she plan? Her mind was blank. I should have talked them out of it, she thought.

Three

To discourage further questions from Trina, Lindsey unloaded the dishwasher and set the table for dinner. Piper was already in his usual place waiting beneath her sister's chair.

"Lindsey, I really appreciate the help," Mrs. Warren said, as she entered from the doorway that led to the garage.

"No problem, Mom." Lindsey wondered if she should tell her mother about the committee. Why not? Maybe then her mother would stop worrying about her. "I signed up for the committee to help with Spring Carnival," she said.

"Oh?"

Lindsey could almost feel the questions struggling to be asked, but her mother turned to the cupboard and took down a vase. She arranged a small bouquet of flowers she'd brought home from the florist where she worked. "These will look nice on the table, dear." She placed the vase filled with delicate baby's breath, miniature blue iris, and golden daffodils in the center of the white cloth. "Bringing a little spring inside never hurts," she said, as she admired the flowers.

The slam of a car door in the drive signaled the arrival of Lindsey's father. The scent of pizza permeated the kitchen as he entered with a large flat box. "Ready to eat?" On Monday, Warren family tradition dictated that Dad bring dinner home.

"Starved," Mrs. Warren said.

"You brought pizza?" Trina dashed into the room and peeked into the box on the counter. "All right! Yum. My favorite — pepperoni and mushrooms. Let's eat. I'm starved."

Piper's tail slapped the rungs of a chair in agreement.

"Me, too," Mr. Warren said as he kissed his wife. "Lindsey, how was your day?" he asked. "Trina, did you pass your math test?"

"We didn't get them back yet, Dad," Trina said.

"My day was fine, Dad." Lindsey placed napkins beside the table settings.

"Tell him about your committee, honey." Mrs. Warren opened the refrigerator and took out salad ingredients. "Trina, help me here." Her mother handed her a cucumber and a knife.

"Tell him about Bill," Trina said.

"Who's Bill?" Mr. Warren slipped out of his suit jacket and loosened his tie.

Curiosity was apparent in the gazes directed Lindsey's way. Mrs. Warren stood by the sink with a head of lettuce dripping in her hands. Trina waited with the knife poised over the cucumber. Mr. Warren's suit jacket dangled from one finger. She felt as if she was watching a stop-action movie, each of her family members playing a part.

"He's just a boy from school, who happens to be on the Spring Carnival committee with me. He gave me, Blaine, everyone, a ride home after the meeting today." Lindsey wished they wouldn't look at her like they were right now. Had she been acting so unusual since she and Ross broke up that mention of a new boy deserved this much attention? Perhaps, she acknowledged to herself.

"The rest of my day was regular," she said. "I'll put the pizza in the oven until we're ready to eat."

"The pizza. I forgot all about it," Mrs. Warren said, in motion again.

Trina and her mother finished the salad. Mr. Warren went to change his clothes. Lindsey turned the oven dial to Warm and slid the pizza inside. She was glad to have a family who cared about her, but being the focus of attention wasn't all that comfortable.

During dinner she expected further questions about Bill and the carnival, but the conversation took a different turn and no one mentioned school again. Mealtime seemed normal at last. Lindsey was relieved.

When she'd finished eating, Lindsey blotted her mouth with a napkin. "Your turn to do dishes, Trina," she said, then left the table, smiling at the face her sister made.

In her room, she emptied her book bag onto her bed and was trying to decide whether to tackle chemistry or modern literature homework first, when the phone rang. "Hello?" Lindsey tucked the receiver between her ear and shoulder.

"May I speak with Lindsey, please?"

"Speaking." Lindsey sat on the edge of her bed.

"This is co-chairperson Bill. How are the kissing booth plans coming?"

"You'll find out when we have the carnival," she said.

"I'll have to wait all that time?"

"Absolutely." Maybe longer, she thought, if I don't think of some unique way to run one.

"There should be some privileges for being a co-chairperson," he grumbled.

"But you aren't co-chairperson of the kissing booth," Lindsey couldn't help saying.

"Well, then how about having a little pity and going out for a hamburger Friday night? Even if you won't let me in on your secret plans, we should discuss a few other details regarding the carnival," he added.

Lindsey hesitated. Couldn't they discuss

the carnival at school? There'd be another meeting next Monday. There was plenty of time.

"Are you there?" Bill asked.

"Yes."

"Great. I'll pick you up about seven."

"I. . . ." She'd meant yes she was there, not yes she'd go.

"If you change your mind and want to discuss those kissing booth plans, we can do that on Friday, too." His voice sounded deeper, sexier.

"No!" She hadn't meant to speak so emphatically, but the way he'd said that had sounded — had sounded — Lindsey's face felt warm as she realized she'd reacted as if he'd been talking about kissing *her*.

"All right. It's your project. See you at school."

"See you," Lindsey answered. They both hung up.

Lindsey opened her chemistry book. "The Pauli Exclusion principle states that in an atom no two electrons can have the same set of quantum numbers," she read. Neutrons, protons, electrons — information she had to know for the test next week was all there. And besides studying, there were the formulas due tomorrow. She stared at the page, seeing only a jumble of black on white. Rather than reading further, she was picturing Bill Stark and remembering how his voice sounded. She shook her head and tried to get involved in her homework. It was no use. She couldn't study here. "Time to head to the library where there aren't any distractions," she said to herself.

The phone rang again.

"Hi, Blaine," said Lindsey as soon as she lifted the receiver.

"Hi, babe. Know who this is?"

For a minute Lindsey couldn't answer. Definitely not Blaine, she thought, staring at the telephone. A confusion of emotions raced through her. "Hello, Ross," she finally said in the most even tones she could manage.

"How are you, Lin?"

"Busy. I was just starting my homework."

"Yeah. Well, are you busy Friday?"

Lindsey held the receiver away from her for a minute. Was he asking her out? Or did he just want to know if she was dating anyone? "Yes. I am," she said.

"So get unbusy. We shouldn't have let 'us' split. What do you say?"

"Did Ruthanne turn you down?"

"I miss *you*, babe." His voice was soft.

Lindsey was tempted. It would be so easy to tell Bill that something came up. Maybe Ross had changed.

"Cancel whatever you were going to do. I'll pick you up around eight. We'll go to Frannie's and then to the show. Wear your pink outfit."

"You have it all planned, Ross — even what I'm supposed to wear?" How could she have thought he'd changed?

"Come on, babe. You know I didn't mean

you had to wear pink. Ross and Lindsey. We look good together. We were a team. Remember? There were lots of good times — the Valentine Dance, Spring Carnival last year. . . ."

Lindsey closed her eyes. Ross knew her well; he knew how to get to her. Spring Carnival last year was when they'd officially started going together. The first time he kissed her had been after the Valentine Dance.

"Decide, babe. I have homework to do, too."

"I can't on Friday, Ross." She hesitated. "How about Saturday or Sunday?"

"Sorry, babe. Friday was when I wanted to see you."

"Then I guess you're out of luck. I have homework to do, too."

"Well, we all have bad luck now and then. See you around school. Think about Friday. You might change your mind." He hung up before she could respond.

Lindsey dropped the receiver back in place, and pushed her hands through her hair. She was shaking, but she wasn't sure whether from anger or the pain of hearing Ross's familiar voice. Maybe a bit of both, she thought, getting up from her bed. She couldn't concentrate on her books right now.

She went to her closet and pulled out the hanger with the pink outfit. As quickly, she jammed it back on the rod. "He's impossible!" she said. "He'll never understand."

She grabbed her light spring jacket off the

hook and her books from the bed. "Mom," she called as she hurried down the stairs, "may I borrow your car to go to the library?"

"If you aren't too late, dear," her mother answered.

"Thanks. I won't be."

The phone shrilled once more. Lindsey hesitated. What if it was Ross calling again? What if he'd changed his mind and wanted her to go out on Saturday or Sunday? It would mean he really did want to see her. It would mean he'd given in to her. She stood with her hand on the front doorknob. The ringing stopped. Lindsey yanked the door open and hurried out.

A couple of moments later, Trina ran out the door behind her. "The phone is for you," she called, waving her arm.

Lindsey started the car and pretended not to hear as she drove the old Pinto away from the front of the house. If Ross wanted to talk to her, he could find her at school. He'd had his chance.

The library wasn't crowded. Lindsey chose a table near the nonfiction shelves. Concentration was as difficult here as it had been at home. I should have waited to find out who was on the phone, she thought, as she idly turned pages in her chemistry book.

"Ahem!"

Lindsey looked up. "What are you doing here, Blaine?"

"I'm looking for you. I called and called your house, but the line was busy. Then when

I got through, I just missed you. Why did you come to the library to do your homework? I haven't forgotten about a term paper or something, have I?"

"No. I couldn't concentrate at home." Lindsey wondered if she sounded disappointed. She couldn't tell. She didn't even know if she felt disappointed to find out that the call she'd missed was from Blaine.

"You couldn't get anything done because of the phone ringing. Right?"

Lindsey nodded.

Blaine sat across from her. "Lin? What's wrong? You seem worried."

Lindsey sighed. "Bill asked me to go out for a hamburger Friday night."

"And that's worrying you? He's not that bad. Did you say you'd go?"

"Mm-hm."

"You sound as if he asked you to go to a funeral."

"Ross called, too." Lindsey's lowered voice was almost a whisper.

"What!" Blaine's voice was unexpectedly loud and she clamped her hand over her mouth. "Did you say what I thought you said? Ross Jordani called you?" she asked in quieter tones.

"Yes."

"What did *he* want?"

"He asked me out Friday night, too."

"Lindsey, you didn't. . . ."

Lindsey rolled her pencil between the palms of her hands. "Almost," she said.

"What do you mean — almost?"

"I said I couldn't on Friday but suggested Saturday or Sunday."

"Oh, Lindsey." Blaine sounded disappointed.

"Don't get upset. He said he'd planned for Friday. We aren't going out at all." A large tear escaped from the corner of her eye and trickled down her face. She brushed it away.

"Do you still love him?" Blaine asked softly.

"I don't know, Blaine." Lindsey searched her purse for a tissue. She blotted her eyes. "I know how he is. And he hasn't changed one bit. But the memories. We had some good times together, and I remember those. I had a boyfriend, someone who loved me. We were a couple. Ross is good-looking. Other girls envied me. Maybe I shouldn't have been so eager to throw that away."

Blaine coughed but didn't say anything.

"I guess I haven't completely let go, even though I was the one who started the break-up. If I hadn't —"

"You'd be running along right behind him. Give yourself time, Lin. I'm here when you want to talk. I haven't been in love yet, but I have a sympathetic ear."

"Thanks, Blaine."

"So, you're going out with Bill?"

"Not really going out. We have to discuss some details about the carnival."

"Um-hm. Well, when you go on this, uh,

business date, could you try not to come on so strong? You were building a soap box skyscraper this afternoon at the meeting."

"What do you mean? I didn't say that much. But someone has to make people aware. I wasn't before, but now I am."

"But you came on so argumentative. 'That's sexist!' 'Chairperson!' When you shove something down people's throats, they tend to choke."

"That sounds very philosophical, Blaine."

"It's not. It's common sense. Just use some."

"What do you want me to say? 'I'd be glad to be your co-chairman'?"

"Semantics are unimportant. If it matters a lot to you, say something like: I'm glad to be co-chairperson. Use the word in an ordinary tone of voice. At the meeting you were either muttering under your breath or lecturing."

"I was not!"

"Lin, you were. You can set the goals of equality back instead of making others aware. When people lecture you, what do you do? Think about it. You tune them out."

Lindsey forgot about Ross and her tears. "All right. I agree about the co-chairperson. I did sound as if I had a chip on my shoulder. But I don't think a smile and soft words were appropriate for a beauty contest, a belly dance, or a kissing booth."

"Lin, it's not *what* you're saying, it's how

you're saying it. Let's not argue. I just thought I should mention that you came on a little strong."

"Okay. You mentioned it."

"How are the plans for the kissing booth coming along?"

"They're not."

"But you're in charge."

"Well, I'm not a miracle worker. And I have homework." Lindsey pulled her chemistry book toward her. "Anyway, as I told Bill, you'll all find out about the kissing booth when the time comes for the carnival."

"But you have to discuss your plans with the committee. And Mr. Harley has to give his approval." Blaine opened her book, too.

"I'll get Mr. Harley's approval. And the kids who are going to work at the booth will know how it's going to operate. For everyone else, the kissing booth is going to be a surprise." And probably for me, too, Lindsey thought, if I don't come up with a good idea.

"I volunteer to work at the booth," said Blaine.

"I thought you were in charge of food."

"I'll do both."

"I'll think about it."

"Lindsey, I'll die of curiosity. Give me one or two little hints about what you're planning. I won't tell anyone. Honest."

Lindsey smiled. "You're as bad as Bill Stark."

"What do you mean?"

"I think he asked me to this special co-chairperson meeting Friday just to find out about the kissing booth."

"Is he going to find out? And can I guess how?"

"He isn't going to find out," Lindsey said firmly, and she hoped the warmth she felt on her face didn't mean she was blushing.

"We'll see." Blaine smirked.

"No, we won't. Have you done your chemistry homework or studied for the test?"

"No. And you're trying to change the subject. Count on a phone call from me on Saturday."

"I might not be home."

"Where might you be?"

Thoughts of Ross flooded back, darkening Lindsey's mood once more. "Nowhere," she said.

"Lin, I lied."

"What?"

"I lied. I did the first chemistry formula." Blaine turned her notebook around to show her.

Lindsey guessed that her friend was trying to cheer her up. "Keep working. We have to do them all. When we're finished we can compare answers." She wrote the first formula on her paper. Across from her, Blaine frowned and chewed on the end of her pencil.

"Write the following formulas," she read silently. Too bad there isn't a formula for love, she thought. Lindsey sighed and tried to concentrate on her homework.

F*our*

Ross was lounging against Lindsey's locker when she arrived at school the next morning. "Hi, babe," he said. His smile accentuated the dimple in his left cheek. His blond hair waved perfectly. Lindsey had no doubt that he was one of the most handsome boys at Woodcreek.

"Hi, Ross." She wished her heart wouldn't beat so rapidly. They weren't going together anymore. She shouldn't react this way when she saw him.

Blaine stood across the hall watching. Lindsey tried not to look in her direction.

"About this weekend —"

"Ross, I told you, I have plans for Friday."

"I know you said that, but, babe —" He put his hands on her shoulders.

She glanced up at him.

"Won't you change them for me?"

"Lindsey, we still have to read over that

chemistry," Blaine called, even though they'd finished the chemistry together last night.

John and Monica passed in the hall. "Hi, Blaine, Lindsey." Monica turned and waved.

"How's the kissing booth coming along, Lindsey? Are you practicing?" John called. His laughter followed.

They were both out of sight before Lindsey could think of an answer.

"Kissing booth?" Ross asked. "What's that all about?"

"I'm on the Spring Carnival committee and in charge of the kissing booth."

"On the committee?" He shrugged. "Well, they were right. We could practice. How about it, babe? Back together Friday for a little practice?"

Lindsey felt pulled in two directions. Part of her struggled against going back to Ross. Yet there was another part that wanted to crawl into his arms and be secure there. A war seemed to be going on inside her head. She was vaguely aware of other students passing in the hall, some turning to look.

"I'll meet you by the library," Blaine called. "Hurry, Lin. We don't have much time."

"Tell her you don't have any time, babe." Ross smiled confidently.

Lindsey forced herself to turn away from him. Her fingers fumbled with the combination on her locker. "My plans are made. I can't change them. And that includes right now. I have to meet Blaine." Her voice sounded like a monotone to her ears. She wished she could start over and say the words as if she really meant them.

"You can't change your plans, or you won't?" Ross took a step back.

She glanced at him. His smile was gone. "Both. It's the same old argument; don't you see that? It has to be your way. Everything has to center around you." Her words sounded stronger this time.

"My way was good enough for a long time." The softness was gone from his voice.

"I know that. But I'm a different person now. I'm me."

"This was Blaine's idea. Right? She never did like me."

"Blaine had nothing to do with our breaking up," Lindsey said indignantly.

"You're selfish, Lindsey. You care only about yourself. You don't care about me. I wonder if you ever did."

Lindsey dropped her books and turned to stare at Ross. "*I'm* selfish? I care only about myself?" She struggled to keep her voice low when she felt like shouting. "You'll never understand, Ross." She stooped to pick up the books. When she straightened up again, he was gone.

The first bell rang. Lindsey hurried to the library. Why was Ross doing this to her? She felt torn apart.

"Are you okay?" Blaine was waiting inside the doorway.

"No, I'm not." Lindsey could hear the

tremble in her voice. "I think he wants to get back together."

"And what do you want?"

Lindsey took a deep breath. "I don't think I want to. I know I'd be taking a dozen steps backward. And yet — oh, Blaine, I wish I'd never loved Ross."

"I don't think you did. Not really. Let's go outside until the last bell rings."

"Of course I did," Lindsey said, as they walked toward the exit.

Outside, they sat on the edge of a brick planter filled with dwarf junipers.

Blaine tilted her head back to soak up the sun. She closed her eyes. "If you truly loved Ross, you'd still be going together. You were attracted to each other. My mom calls it puppy love. She says that kind of love is sort of practice for the real thing. You find out what it's like to be close to someone and share fun, but it's not the real thing." She changed positions and scuffed the bottom of her tennis shoe across the pavement. She looked serious.

"It sure seemed real. If it wasn't, why do I feel so awful when I think about Ross? Why am I so torn up inside when he calls me babe and says he wants to get back together?" The piney aroma of juniper scented the air as Lindsey snapped off the end of a branch and shredded it into tiny blue-green slivers.

"Because you're still scared of being without a boyfriend. If you really loved each other, you wouldn't both be trying to change each other. You'd accept him for the selfish, egotistical person he is and . . ."

"Blaine!"

Others lounging in front of school, enjoying as much spring as possible before going inside, turned to look at them.

Lindsey lowered her voice. "He isn't that bad."

"And he'd be glad that you want to grow as a person, be involved, have an opinion. He'd even encourage you. And you'd encourage him to do the same," Blaine continued as if she hadn't heard Lindsey's defense.

"I did encourage him."

"It takes two to make love work."

"You sound like a mother."

"I can't help it. My mom and I have been having some serious discussions lately, since — well, since I've become interested in Ryan."

"I still feel very confused." Lindsey brushed the juniper slivers off her lap and rubbed her hands together.

Blaine nodded. "I know. Give yourself time, Lin."

"Time. I gave myself plenty of that when I broke up with Ross."

The second bell rang to signal the impending start of first period classes. Nearby, students turned toward the entrance. Lindsey and Blaine picked up their books and did the same.

"Meet me for lunch," said Blaine as they went up the steps.

Lindsey nodded.

They both headed for class.

Lindsey was walking with her head down, lost in thought, when she felt a hand on her arm. She jumped.

"I didn't mean to scare you." Bill Stark fell into step beside her. "Would you have lunch with me? I think we can do a dunk tank for the carnival. If I can round up the committee, I want to show everyone my plan."

"I'm meeting Blaine for lunch. I'll tell her. Where will you sit?"

"Let's try for a table near the back right side of the cafeteria. You have first lunch period, don't you?"

"Juniors and seniors. First lunch."

"Good. I have to catch up with the others. See you then."

"See you." Lindsey stopped outside her English class and watched him stride away. Today he wore a dark green sweater. The color looked good on him, she thought, hurrying into the room to her first row desk, where she forced herself to pay attention. If she didn't, she'd be in the junior part of juniors and seniors again next year.

Alicia was already at a table when Blaine and Lindsey reached the cafeteria. She'd put a book at each place to reserve them. She waved.

Lindsey waved back.

"Aah. You can tell from that intense, pukey

aroma that today's cafeteria special is tuna surprise. And I'd be real surprised if there was any tuna in the tuna surprise," John said, as he and Monica stepped into line behind them.

"There're always grilled cheese sandwiches," Blaine said.

"By graduation, I'll be talking with a squeaky voice, growing extra-long whiskers on my face, and have developed a great fear of cats," he said.

"John always eats grilled cheese," Monica explained. "I keep telling him to bring his lunch like I do, but I guess he's too lazy."

"What a nag! You sound like my mother," John said, but he ruffled her hair affectionately.

They quickly passed the steam table displaying the special of the day.

Monica bought milk while the rest bought grilled cheese sandwiches.

"Did you eat already, Alicia?" Blaine asked when they put their trays on the table.

"My old stand-by — peanut butter and jelly."

"That sounds wonderful," John said. "Wish I'd thought to bring the same."

"Do you want half of my turkey sandwich?" Monica asked. "I'm dieting anyway and don't need it all."

"No. I'll struggle through my usual," John said.

Ryan and Bill were the last to arrive.

"They have my favorite today," Bill said. "Tuna surprise."

The rest of them groaned.

"I like it, too," Ryan said. "What's wrong with it?"

"Don't tell him until I've finished eating," Bill said.

Ryan looked from one to the other. "Blaine?"

"It's made from all the good stuff that the starving children in the world would love to eat," she said.

"Seaweed?" Ryan asked.

Bill choked.

"That's one I never heard before," John said. "What do you eat at your house?"

"I'm sure I read someplace that they were trying to make food from seaweed so people wouldn't starve. No?" Ryan looked from one person to another.

"You mean your mother never told you to finish something you didn't like because all the starving children in the world would love to have it?" Lindsey asked. She wiped her mouth and fingers with a napkin and opened her milk carton.

"My mother never had to ask me to finish. I like everything," Ryan said. "I was one of the starving children."

"Me, too," Bill said. "My mother told me if I'd eat everything, I'd grow big and tall. She was right."

"We shouldn't joke, you know," Alicia said.

"It's true that millions of children do go to bed hungry in this world. That's not a myth made up by parents to make their children eat. That's pretty sad."

No one said any more about tuna surprise, and Ryan went back to eating his lunch.

"If some of you are finished, look at this." Bill reached under his chair and pulled a paper from inside his notebook. Monica spread the paper out in the center of the table.

"What is this?" John pointed to a diagram of a round circle, some waves, and a stick figure.

"A dunk tank," Bill said.

"Mr. Harley won't let us have that in the gym." Alicia came around the table to study the drawing.

Bill finished his lunch and explained how the dunk tank would work — outside. "All I have to do is talk my neighbor into letting us use his portable pool. The platform will be easy to build."

"I think it will be super. But will the weather be warm enough by then?" Lindsey asked.

"I have a wet suit." Ryan put his tray under his chair and leaned forward to see the sketch.

"Like frogmen wear?" Blaine asked.

"Like surfers wear," Ryan said.

"That's right! You used to be a California surf bum." John pushed the sketch back to Bill. "I think we have a dunk tank."

Lindsey sat back in her chair. "Not yet we don't."

They all looked at her.

"Who's going to volunteer to be dunked?" she asked.

Monica pointed at John. John pointed at Alicia. Alicia pointed at Ryan. Ryan pointed at Blaine. Blaine pointed at Lindsey.

"Not me," Lindsey said. "You gave me the kissing booth to run. The dunk tank is Bill's idea." She couldn't resist smiling as they all pointed at Bill.

"What if Ryan's wet suit doesn't fit me?" he asked.

"Then you'll freeze." Alicia sounded very matter-of-fact.

"One of you girls could always sit on the platform and keep him warm," John suggested.

"All those in favor of John taking turns with Bill raise a hand." Monica put her hand up.

John looked shocked. "What? And get pneumonia? Would you take care of me if I got sick, Monica?"

"Sure. I'd bring you tuna surprise." She patted his arm.

"Bill, the dunk tank is all yours," John said.

"Maybe we should all take turns?" Bill looked hopeful.

"Maybe we can get one of the teachers to volunteer," Ryan suggested.

"Ryan! Great thinking," Blaine said. "Mr. Devine, the PE coach, for instance."

"Yes!" the others echoed enthusiastically. Ryan stood up and bowed.

"Who's going to ask?" Alicia wondered.

They all pointed at Bill.

"Asking can't hurt," he said. "I'll put the dunk tank on the list of ideas to present to Mr. Harley. I wonder if he'd . . . ?"

"Asking can't hurt," Lindsey repeated.

"You'll be right there with me," Bill said. "Co-chairpeople see Mr. Harley together."

Everyone laughed.

The bell rang for the next period and the start of junior and senior afternoon classes.

Lindsey found herself walking beside Bill on the way out of the cafeteria. "Don't forget Friday night," he said.

"You mean there's more to discuss?" she asked.

Bill smiled. "Lots more."

Lindsey was smiling back, when Ross and Ruthanne passed them in the hall. Her arm was possessively twined around his. Ross acted as if he didn't even see Lindsey. She glanced away and tried to concentrate on what Bill was saying about the carnival. She no longer felt like smiling.

Afternoon classes were over, and Lindsey returned to her locker. When she opened the door, a piece of paper fluttered to her feet. The jagged scrawl she recognized as Ross's covered two lines.

"One last chance, she read. How about Friday?" She looked around, but there was no sign of Ross. She crumpled the paper and threw it in the bottom of her locker. What she didn't need from Ross was more ultimatums.

"Ready?" Blaine asked.

"What? Oh, yeah. I'll be ready in a minute." Lindsey glanced at her friend. Her skin looked flushed and the grin on her face would have set a record for width. "Either you have a stomachache and a fever, or something good has happened," she said.

"My stomach never felt better, but I do feel warm all over." Blaine laughed. "Ryan asked me to go out Friday. He asked for my phone number, too."

"Oh, Blaine, that's super!"

"Now we both have a date for Friday, Lin."

"Both?" She thought of the note she'd just crumpled.

"You're going out with Bill; I'm going out with Ryan."

"I don't have a date. Bill just wants to discuss the carnival. He even reminded me after lunch."

"That's right. Now I remember. Business." Blaine tried to look serious. "Do you really believe that, Lindsey?"

"I have no reason not to," she said, determined not to consider the possibility that Bill had asked her for any other reason. After all,

she wasn't interested in boys; and after today, she thought that was a good decision.

Outside, the air was balmy. Lindsey looked
up at the trees with their newly sprung
miniature leaves. Even the brown lawns
seemed to have a hint of green poking from
beneath the moist soil.

"Now I know why the poets write about
spring and love in the same sentence," Blaine
said. "Remember that line about a young
man's thoughts?"

"You worry about Ryan's thoughts," Lindsey said. "Bill and I are going to discuss the
carnival."

"Whatever you say, Lin," Blaine said
agreeably. "I'm not in the mood to argue with
anyone about anything." She hugged her
book bag and sighed. "Spring is my absolute
favorite time of year."

Lindsey tried to smile, but it hurt. So far
this spring hadn't been so wonderful for her.

Five

The rest of the week passed quickly for Lindsey, though Blaine complained that time dragged.

On Friday, in the back of the bus, Blaine talked nonstop about her date with Ryan that evening.

"I've tried on every outfit in my closet," she said. "I've decided on the blue jumpsuit. What do you think?"

"Hmm?"

"I said I thought I'd go naked on my date tonight."

"You're what?"

Blaine poked Lindsey and laughed. "You obviously were not listening to me."

Lindsey sighed. "I'm sorry. What did you say?"

Blaine repeated her choice of clothes.

"You'll look fine," Lindsey said. "Wear that

wraparound belt you have instead of the little blue tie."

"Are you sure?"

"Yes. Let it ride on your hips."

"I've already got too much riding on my hips."

"You've lost at least ten pounds since Christmas. You look good, Blaine."

"I know. I just like to hear someone tell me every now and then. What are you going to wear tonight?"

Lindsey shrugged.

"Pink?"

"No!" Lindsey snapped.

"What did I say?" Blaine looked wide-eyed.

"Nothing. It's my fault. I didn't mean to yell. It's just that Ross suggested I wear my pink outfit when he asked me to change my plans and go out with him."

"Forget Ross. If you want to wear pink, wear pink. If you don't, don't."

Lindsey nodded. "You're right. Maybe I will — if I want to."

"What's wrong? Are you nervous about tonight?"

"Nervous? Of course not." Lindsey slid down in the bus seat. "Yes, I am. It's so stupid. There's nothing special about tonight. But I'm scared, Blaine."

"Me, too."

"But you have a reason. This is your first date with Ryan (and you like him, and. . . .)"

"And we'll both be fine," Blaine reassured her.

"Yeah. We will. I guess it's just because I haven't gone anyplace with anyone but Ross in a long time. Who does Bill date, anyway?" Lindsey asked.

Blaine smiled. "Why do you want to know?"

"I'm just curious. And don't look at me like that."

"Like what?"

"As if you think I'm interested in Bill. I'm not. I was only wondering about him, that's all."

"I know. No more boys. Bill used to go with Alexis Lane."

"Used to?"

"She moved to Texas last summer."

"Oh."

"And no one has replaced her."

"Stop it, Blaine."

"Stop what?"

"You know what. You're doing it again."

"You asked me; I didn't ask you."

"This is my stop." Lindsey was glad to see the familiar street sign.

"I'll call you in the morning," Blaine said.

Lindsey waved and jumped off the bottom bus step. She didn't rush home, however. She walked slowly and tried to talk her stomach out of the crazy flip-flops it kept doing every time she thought about her date with Bill. "You'd think I'd never gone anywhere with a boy before," she scolded herself.

When Lindsey entered her room, Trina was sitting on her bed, leafing through a teen fashion magazine. Piper was on the floor, and he rolled over, hinting he wanted to be petted.

Lindsey bent down and scratched his stomach.

"Bill called." Trina tried to imitate one of the model's poses.

"Bill? What did he want?" Lindsey stood up, and Piper protested before dropping his head onto his paws and closing his eyes.

"Don't look so worried."

"I'm not. Trina, what did he want?"

"Just to tell you he'd be coming at seven-thirty instead of seven o'clock. I didn't know you were going out with him." Trina stretched out across the bed. She was posing again.

"I'm not."

"But he said. . . ."

"We're having a business meeting."

"Oh. Then you are going out. Do Mom and Dad know?"

"Not yet. What are you doing in my room?"

"Answering the phone and looking at your magazine. You won't be eating with us tonight, will you?"

"I — I guess not."

Trina jumped off the bed. "Don't forget it's your turn to set the table. You could do it now. Come on, Piper."

"It's only four o'clock."

"I know. If you want me to do it for you, I'll trade clearing the table tomorrow. Deal?"

"Deal," Lindsey said.

Trina started out of the room with the dog at her heels. She backtracked. "Lin, will I get to meet Bill? He has a sexy voice."

"Trina!"

"Geez, Lindsey. He does. You should hear him on the phone."

"I have." Lindsey couldn't help but smile.

"Well, don't worry; I won't try to steal him — at least not tonight," Trina said.

Lindsey laughed.

Trina looked indignant. "You think I'm a little kid, but I'm not, Lin. I'm in seventh grade. So if you don't like Bill — "

"I don't like any boys."

"He doesn't sound like a boy; he sounds like a man. In fact, if I didn't love that dreamy movie star Rob Lowe so much, I might flirt with Bill tonight when he comes to pick you up."

"Flirt away, Trina. I told you, this is a business meeting — about the carnival."

"Maybe he's going to ask you to be his date."

"We're both working on the carnival."

"If you say so, Lin."

A door slammed. "Hello! Where is everyone?" Mrs. Warren called from downstairs.

"Up here," Trina answered. "Mom must have got off work early today. Are you going to tell her about your date — I mean your meeting — now?"

"You can tell her." Lindsey took off her sweater and hung it in the closet.

Trina and Piper were gone again. "Mom, guess what?" echoed back from the stairway.

Lindsey couldn't hear the rest of what her sister said. She took out her pink cotton skirt and blouse.

"Is that what you're going to wear tonight?" Lindsey's mother asked from the doorway.

"I might." Lindsey put the outfit on her bed.

"Pink is your color. Is this boy you're going out with the same boy who is on the committee with you?"

"Yes. Didn't Trina tell you?"

"She said that you have a date with Bill."

"Not a date, Mom. A business meeting. He asked me to go out and discuss the carnival plans." Lindsey was getting tired of explaining to everyone.

Her mother nodded. "I'm glad you aren't sitting home feeling sorry for yourself over Ross." This was the first time her mother had spoken about the break-up. "What time are you leaving?"

"Around seven-thirty. Trina said she was going to tell you."

"I told her I wanted to hear about it from you." Her mother came into the room and sat on the edge of the bed. "I've been worried about you, Lin, but I didn't want to pry. You and Ross dated for a long time."

"Not quite a year, Mom."

"Do you want to talk about him — about anything?"

Lindsey shook her head. "Not now, Mom. Do you mind?"

Her mother sighed. "I'm willing to listen."

Lindsey sat beside her. "I know, Mom. But I'm trying to forget about Ross. I'm trying to get back to being me without him."

Her mother nodded. "Your dad and I are here when you need us. We feel left out, honey."

"I'm sorry. This is something I have to handle myself, Mom. You can't help. I'm not a little girl anymore."

Her mother patted her hand. "I know. But please remember, we'll always listen if you want to talk."

"Thanks, Mom. I'll remember. But sometimes talking won't help or change anything. Sometimes you just need time. I'll be okay." And I will be, Lindsey thought, as long as I keep busy and Ross leaves me alone.

"Bill and I are going out for hamburgers, so I won't be eating with you."

"Trina did tell me that." Her mother smiled and stood up. "I'll leave you to plan what you want to wear."

Lindsey picked up the hanger with her pink outfit on it. "I think I will wear this," she said.

Lindsey was ready early and sat in the living room waiting. The doorbell rang at twenty after seven.

"I'll get it." Trina ran to answer. She'd changed into new jeans and a blue blouse.

She'd also unbraided her hair and pulled it into a wavy pony tail, which hung to her waist.

Lindsey noticed that her younger sister looked older tonight. She followed Trina to the door. "Hi, Bill. Come in," she said.

"Hi." He looked nice in jeans and a brown suede jacket over an off-white sweater.

"This is my sister Trina. Trina, Bill Stark."

"Hi, Trina. We talked earlier." Bill smiled.

"Hi. I knew who you were." Trina leaned against the front door and smiled back at him.

Piper came running from the kitchen. He barked and wagged his tail.

"Who's this?" Bill asked, stooping down and holding out his hand.

Piper sniffed and nudged Bill to be petted. Bill accommodated by scratching behind his ears.

"That's Piper," Lindsey said. "Trina, would you put him back in the kitchen, please?"

"Don't take him away on my account," Bill said. "Right, boy? We're friends, aren't we?"

Piper's agreement was obvious from the tip of his nose to the tip of his tail; all of him was wagging now. Happy sounds came from deep in his throat.

"He really does like you," Trina said. The glance she gave Lindsey said, *not like Ross*.

Bill stood up after giving Piper one last

pat. "He's a nice dog. You should enter him in the contest."

"What contest?" Trina asked.

"It's a secret," Lindsey said. "Part of the carnival. You'll find out when we do the publicity."

"Bill, tell me?" Trina pleaded.

"Mm-mm. Your sister's right. We can't give you the advantage over other entrants."

"I can't wait to find out," Trina said.

Bill smiled then winked at Lindsey.

She smiled back." My mom and dad are in the living room. Come and meet them, Bill." Lindsey led the way.

Trina followed after them, keeping a hold on Piper's collar.

After introductions, Bill and Lindsey's dad talked for a couple of minutes about the carnival, a tradition at Woodcreek High.

"If I can help out with the food or anything at all, let me know. Friendly's is what it's name says." Her father laughed as he quoted the store slogan.

"We'll surely take you up on your offer, Mr. Warren. Thanks." Bill turned to Lindsey. "Ready?"

She nodded and put her coat on before Bill could help her with it. "We won't be late," she said as they walked toward the front door. "I have my key."

"Have fun," Trina said, she and Piper still trailing after them.

"We'll try," Bill said. "It was nice meeting all of you."

"Hope we see you again," Trina called as they went down the front walk. Piper barked his agreement.

Lindsey turned around, but Trina was closing the door.

"Your sister's a cute kid," Bill said.

Lindsey nodded. "Do you have any brothers or sisters?"

"An older sister. She's married and lives up in Traverse City. But I can sympathize with Trina."

"What do you mean, sympathize?" Lindsey slid onto the front seat of the station wagon. "Sympathy is one thing my sister doesn't seem to need."

"I can't believe that. Everyone knows that big sisters pick on their siblings."

"Everyone does not know that. In fact, I'd say, from experience, that it's often the other way around. And I bet if I talked to your sister, she'd agree."

"What? Never!" Bill laughed, started the car, and pulled away from the curb. "I've always been the perfect little brother."

Lindsey cleared her throat. "I knew you in junior high. Remember?"

"No." Bill glanced at her. "What do you remember about me in junior high?"

"I was a student council rep for seventh grade when you were rep for eighth grade."

"Ah, yes. Eighth grade. The year of — "

" — Mr. Moriarity," they both said together and laughed. "Do you remember — ?" they said once more in unison.

"Mr. Moriarity's suggestion box," Lindsey said. "Wasn't there a contest to see who could put the most outrageous suggestion in without getting caught?"

Bill laughed and shook his head. "Some of those suggestions must have been unrepeatable."

"I have a feeling you know which ones," said Lindsey.

"Me?"

Lindsey nodded. "You never did take anything seriously."

"Wrong," Bill said. "You didn't know me very well."

"Stark the Spark?"

"An act. And the name wasn't my choice."

"An act? What for?"

"It's a long story. Let's just say that I was feeling insecure. Anyway, Moriarity's suggestion box disappeared before the end of first semester. Remember?" Bill asked, changing the subject back to their original conversation.

"His year as vice-principal of Farmington Meadows Junior High must have gone down in a record book somewhere."

"As what? The torturer or the torturee?" Bill asked. "I recall his famous subtract this number punishment: one number that filled the whole top line of a paper — subtract 39 until you get to zero or a number less than 39. Pages of math. No wonder it's my least favorite subject."

"I only had to do that once. But do you remember his junkmobile?"

"Vividly," said Bill.

"Doesn't Mike Milburg drive it now?" Lindsey asked.

"Hey! Mike is known for his love of that old clunker he drives. No. I think Mr. Moriarity's car was worse than Mike's any day."

"The kids decorated it at the end of the school year. I heard you were the one who glued erasers to the hubcaps." Lindsey glanced at Bill's profile, visible in the shadowy light cast by the streetlights they passed. Her grandmother would have said he had a strong chin. Funny how strange phrases like that came to you at weird times, she thought.

Bill laughed. "I suppose you were always good in junior high?"

"Not always. I got sent out of home arts because I wanted to cook, not watch the teacher do everything. And I wanted to know how to make things from scratch, not out of a box."

"Militant even then, huh?"

"What do you mean, militant?"

"Combative, fighting, aggressive." Bill stopped the car at a light. "Right, co-chairperson?"

"Sneer if you must, Bill Stark; but I've learned that some people take advantage and walk all over you, if you aren't a little militant."

"You said the key word, Lindsey — some."

She wished she could see the look in his eyes because his voice suddenly sounded serious. But the light had changed, and he was looking at the road. A few minutes later he turned the car into the lot at Frannie's Pantry. As usual, the restaurant was jammed.

"We might have to wait for a table," Bill said as he opened the heavy glass door.

"No we won't. Someone is leaving — there." Lindsey pointed at a booth for two where a couple were putting on jackets.

The restaurant was painted blue; the booths were rust-colored vinyl. Posters of Michigan scenery decorated the walls. The scent of grilled hamburgers and onions tinged the air. The buzz of conversation and the clink of silverware was overpowered by the beat of rock music pouring from a speaker. At the back was the famous signature wall, where people were encouraged to sign their names, an effort to counteract graffiti elsewhere.

As soon as the other couple left, Bill guided Lindsey toward the booth. A bus boy was clearing the table when they got there. He looked up, brushed black curls away from his eyes, and smiled. "Hi, Bill. Hi, Lindsey."

"Hi, Mike," Bill said. "I didn't know you worked here." He winked at Lindsey.

"Just started, but work is the word. This place is a zoo; the pay is bare minimum; but it's a job and will help keep my wreck running."

"Whatever it takes when you have your own car," Bill teased.

"Right. One of these days I'll get ahead enough to fix her up. Jennifer will be here in a minute to take your order." He picked up the plastic tub he used to clear dishes and went to another table.

They ordered and were waiting for their hamburgers to come. Lindsey looked around. Many of the customers were kids from school; there were also some young families. Her gaze drifted back to Bill, and she was startled to find him watching her. She glanced away again, looking toward the door. "Oh, no," she said softly.

"Is something wrong?" Bill asked.

"Um, no. Nothing's wrong."

Ross and Ruthanne were coming toward their booth. Her brunette coloring was a contrast to his blondness. Ross's smile faded when he saw Lindsey. He stopped when he reached their table.

"Lindsey," he said, "I was going to call you. Then I remembered that you said you were busy tonight."

"Hi, Ross, Ruthanne." Lindsey tried to keep her voice calm.

"Hi, Lindsey." Ruthanne smiled sweetly at her, then up at Ross. She held tightly to his arm, the top of her head just reaching his shoulder. "Hi, Bill," she added.

"Ruthanne." Bill nodded.

Ross ignored Bill and continued. "I'd like

my photograph back. I'll stop by your house tomorrow to get it."

"I don't know if I'll be home." Lindsey felt the warmth of a blush starting up her neck to her face.

"Trina can give me the photo. You don't have to be there."

Even his tone of voice said *you don't matter*. It was something she'd suspected, but hearing it in not so many words was still a shock. "I'll have to look for it, Ross. I might have thrown it away." Lindsey tried to keep her voice even. "You'd better call before you make a trip for nothing."

"Oh, I hope you didn't throw his picture away." Ruthanne rested her head against Ross. "He promised I could have it."

"Here comes our dinner," Bill said. "Nice seeing you two."

"See you," Ruthanne said, as Ross took her hand and dragged her away without saying good-bye.

Lindsey wrapped her napkin into a ball in her lap. She didn't know where to look. She was glad when the waitress put plates in front of them.

"Finally. We can eat. I'm starved," Bill said. "I hope you didn't lose your appetite. Are you all right?"

Lindsey glanced at him. "I'm fine. I'm hungry." She looked at the steaming hamburger the waitress had put in front of her, and wished that were true. She was furious with herself for letting Ross bother her the way he did.

She ate a little at a time, finally managing to finish the hamburger and her soft drink.

"Let's get out of here," Bill said. "We can talk anyplace."

Lindsey reached for her purse. She pulled out a five dollar bill. "Take mine out of this." She handed the money across the table.

"This time it's on me. You can pay next time," Bill said. "Deal?"

Lindsey nodded and forced herself to walk straight toward the door without looking around.

The air outside felt cool and good on her face. She glanced up at a night sky dotted with stars and inhaled deeply and exhaled slowly. In the car, she and Bill didn't talk. He turned on the radio and drove.

"There's a comedy playing at the Northland I," Bill said. "I heard it's really good. Want to see it?"

"Oh, I — I don't know."

"Well, I do. That's one vote; but since we're co-chairpeople, we need a unanimous decision. How about it?"

"I thought we were going to discuss the carnival."

"We will. Movie? Please?" He looked as pathetic as Piper when he wanted something.

Lindsey had to smile. "All right. But I pay."

"Your share. Agreed." Bill sped up the car

and turned into the mall lot where the theater was located.

"Want some dessert?" he asked as they entered the lobby. "A chocolate bar? Popcorn? Mints?"

"Mints," Lindsey said. "We can share them."

"Deal."

The movie was funny. She laughed and felt better. They shared the mints, then later a box of popcorn.

"That was fun. I'm glad we agreed," he said as they walked back to the car afterward.

"Me, too. Thanks." Lindsey smiled.

"You look good in pink," he said.

"Thanks," she said again and blocked out thoughts of Ross.

While they drove home, Bill told her about almost blowing up the science lab in junior high. "That's when they started calling me Stark the Spark. I think my student file had a warning on it. I haven't been in a chemistry class in high school."

"You haven't! What happened when you signed up?"

"I didn't. I make *me* nervous in chemistry, too. I opted for biology and earth science."

Lindsey laughed.

When they stopped in front of her house, Bill jumped out of the car and came around to her side. He walked with her to the front door. The scent of rich, thawed earth was heavy in the night air.

"Bill, we never discussed the carnival. That's what we were supposed to do," Lindsey said, as she stepped onto the porch. The varnished front door of the neat brick colonial reflected the porch light.

"Well, maybe next weekend we can do that. Can I take you roller skating next Saturday?"

"No. I think you'd better come over here. That way we'll get something done — without distractions."

"Whatever you say. Which day? What time?"

"Saturday. Seven o'clock."

"Fine. See you Monday at the meeting." He ran down the walk to his car, waved, and got in.

Lindsey watched. She felt as if she'd just stepped off a merry-go-round, but the events of the evening continued to spin in a circle in her head. Later in her room, the clock hands moved past midnight before she was able to get to sleep.

Six

"Wake up. We have to talk." The mattress sagged with the weight of someone sitting.

Lindsey opened her eyes.

"Good morning." Blaine was perched on the edge of the bed.

"Morning? Already?" Lindsey yawned. "What time is it?"

"Nine. Your mom said I could wake you up."

"Aargh!" Lindsey rolled over and buried her face in the pillow.

"Did you and Bill stay out late?"

"No."

"Did you discuss a lot of business?"

Lindsey mumbled something she hoped Blaine couldn't understand.

"You didn't talk about the carnival at all."

Lindsey raised her head. "I didn't say that."

Blaine grinned. "But that's what you meant."

"Tell me about Ryan. I know that's why you're here disturbing my beauty rest."

"As if you need any."

"Thanks." Lindsey propped herself up on one elbow and looked at her friend's smiling face. "After a compliment like that, I'm half awake and ready to hear every detail of your date."

Blaine couldn't talk fast enough. She walked back and forth across the bedroom, ending up on the bed again, where she fell back beside Lindsey. "I think I'm in love," she said.

"I think you are, too. I'm glad you had such a good time."

"And he kissed me. Did I tell you that he kissed me?"

"You told me." Lindsey thought about her evening with Bill. She doubted that he had even thought about kissing her.

"Did I say something wrong?" Blaine sat up.

"No."

"You're frowning. Didn't you have fun last night?"

"It was okay. We saw Ross and Ruthanne at Frannie's."

"Uh-oh."

"Ross wants his picture back. He stopped by our table at Frannie's to tell me."

"That sounds like Ross." Blaine looked toward the dresser. "Where is his picture?"

"In my closet."

There was a scratch and whine at the door as Piper nudged it open wide enough to enter.

He was followed by Trina, as wide awake as Blaine and already dressed. "Did you have fun last night?" she asked.

Blaine answered. Lindsey didn't.

The phone rang and Trina answered. "No," she said. "No. Don't . . ." Trina frowned before dropping the receiver back in place. "That was Ross. He says he's coming over to get his picture. He said you knew all about it. I told him no; I even said you weren't here, but he. . . ."

"I can guess. He's coming anyway," Blaine said. "Want to go someplace with me, Lin? If we hurry — "

"No." Lindsey sighed. She opened the closet door, took the picture from her shelf, and slipped the photograph out of the frame. "I should have said I'd mail it to him."

"I can come close. I'll drive past his house on the way home and put it in his mailbox," Blaine said.

Lindsey looked down at the smiling face in the picture. Ross wore the powder blue sweater she'd given him for his birthday and posed with his head turned slightly to the side. The photograph had been his gift to her on her birthday. "No. I'd better give this to him myself."

"If he's coming, then I'm leaving," Trina

said. "And Piper, too. If Mom and Dad come back from shopping, tell them I'm at Kelly's house," she called over her shoulder.

Lindsey turned toward her bed and pulled up the sheets and blanket. She was upset — about Ross coming over, about parting with the photograph, and upset because this upset her.

"Lin, I don't think you should let Ross come over," Blaine said.

"Why not? He might already be on his way. I'll give him the photo and then he'll leave."

"You're still vulnerable."

"The only way I'll get invulnerable is to face him when I have to."

"Aren't you asking an awful lot of yourself? I saw how you looked at his picture."

"His picture isn't him. I can't just stuff the picture in his mailbox. It seems so —"

"Uncaring? Final?" Blaine asked.

"Those are your words. I'll handle everything."

Blaine sighed. "I have to get home. Ryan said he might come over today. I'll call you later."

"Okay. And don't worry."

When Lindsey was alone again, she sat on the bed. Her shoulders slumped forward; she closed her eyes and sighed. "Ross and Lindsey really are over," she whispered. "And I can't sit around feeling sorry for myself."

She jumped up again, finished making her bed, and hurried to take her shower. After breakfast, Lindsey sat with a sheet of paper in front of her, trying to come up with an idea for the booth. She avoided looking at the photograph that rested beside her on the table. But her ears were tuned to the sounds outside. She was waiting for one particular sound — Ross's car.

When she finally heard the screech of brakes in front, she made herself remain seated and waited for the doorbell to ring. She walked slowly to answer.

Ross was sitting on the low wrought iron rail that rimmed the edge of the porch. He was wearing jeans and the blue sweater. "Have you got the picture?" he asked.

"Yes. Wait here. I'll get it."

"Where is everyone?" He stepped past her.

"My parents went shopping. Trina is at a friend's."

"You mean we're alone? Good. We have to talk."

"About what, Ross? There's nothing to say."

"There's plenty to say — about us."

"There is no us."

"That's why we have to talk." He followed her.

"The time for talking is over, Ross." Lindsey hurried to the table and picked up the photo. "Here it is."

"You know me and you love me." He lounged in the doorway, blocking her exit. "Don't you believe in second chances? I do."

"Ross —" She held out the photo.

"Didn't take you long to find someone to take my place, did it?" His words were soft-spoken, but his voice had an edge to it. He put his hands on her shoulders and pulled her toward him.

"I don't know what you mean." Her pulse pounded in her ears.

"Bill Stark," he said sarcastically.

"We're on the carnival committee together, that's all."

"Then you do still love me." He bent to kiss her.

Lindsey pulled away.

Ross looked surprised. "You said no one was home. I only want to kiss you, babe. Then you'll remember how good it was with us."

"I — I don't want you to." She glanced from the picture of Ross to Ross himself.

"Lindsey, we belong together. You belong to me."

She felt tears behind her eyes and swallowed to keep them inside. "You still don't understand, do you?" she asked. "I'm a person, Ross; not a possession. How can there be a *we* if there isn't a *me*? I have to know who I am, before I have anything to offer to someone else."

Ross frowned. "I never complained about what you had to offer."

"Because you didn't care, Ross. As long as you could say, 'This is my girlfriend Lindsey,' that's all that mattered to you. You don't even know the real me."

"That's ridiculous, Lindsey. You talk as if you have a pretty poor opinion of yourself. That sounds like some garbage you read in a book."

"It's not garbage; it's the way I feel, Ross. Here." She handed the picture to him. "Give this to Ruthanne. You were eager to get it back last night and she's eager to have it."

He looked at the photograph. It was hard to tell what he was thinking. "No. I think you should keep it a while longer, babe." He handed it to her, then strolled toward the door. "You'll come back to me, Lindsey," he called. "I know it." The door slammed before she could answer.

Now the tears slipped down her face. Lindsey threw the photograph on the table and fell into the chair. She cradled her head in her arms. Frustration gnawed at her, as well as a little doubt. Was Ross right? Did she want to go back to him? Did it really matter that he demanded all of her time? Would she miss out on that much? Wasn't it more important that they had each other? Wasn't that what love was all about?

She pulled a tissue from her pocket and blew her nose. "He's not right," she said. "At least not yet. I meant what I said. I have to be me." But maybe separation would make them both change and they could get back together sometime. Maybe Ross wasn't entirely wrong. She ran upstairs and shoved the photograph back on the closet shelf.

In the bathroom, she splashed her face with

water. Then she went back to the kitchen where she'd left the blank paper where she hoped to write down some ideas about a kissing booth. She forced Ross out of her mind.

How can I plan a kissing booth where no one kisses anyone? she wondered. She stared at the paper in front of her. The others had suggested a traditional booth with both boys and girls. That would be equal, but — Lindsey tapped her pencil on the paper. If only she could think of something unique.

Trina and Piper burst through the kitchen doorway.

"Look at this, Lin. My absolutely favorite movie star." Trina unrolled a poster of Rob Lowe. "Kelly got a new one and gave me this one."

"What happened to his face?" Lindsey pointed to red smudges.

"Oh, that." Trina giggled. "Those are lip prints from Kelly kissing him."

"Lip prints?"

Trina nodded. "You make them with lipstick. I'm sure you've made lip prints, Lin; but I won't mention on whom."

"Thanks, Trina."

"Oh, you're welcome. Did he come for his picture?"

"What?"

"The person you thanked me for not mentioning."

"He came, but that wasn't what I was thanking you for."

"It wasn't?" Trina sounded confused. "Then why did you say thanks?"

"For sharing your poster with me."

"You like Rob Lowe, too?"

"No. I just like the poster."

"Oh. Well, you can look at it whenever you want. I'm going to tape it to my bedroom door." Trina raced from the room.

Lindsey turned to her paper and wrote: Kissing booth — Buy posters of popular stars and let people kiss their favorites. She tried to picture some of the kids she knew paying money to do this. Filled with doubt as she tried to imagine Alicia or Monica kissing a poster, Lindsey sighed. "I'll mark this plan number one," she muttered. "It's the only thing I can think of right now."

The phone rang.

"I'll get it," she called.

"This is Blaine," said the voice on the other end. "Did Ross come by?"

"Yes."

"Did he ask you out again?"

"No."

"Good. That's over."

Lindsey didn't correct her friend's misconception.

"Listen, do you want to go to the show or the mall or somewhere?"

"I thought Ryan was coming over."

"He's here now. But he has to leave around two."

"I don't think so, Blaine. I'm working on my plans for the carnival."

"You mean for the kissing booth? Call me if you change your mind about going out or about discussing those plans."

"Well, maybe I could bounce one idea off you. It's not my best one . . ."

"What is your best one?"

"I'm working on that one. Just listen to this idea." Lindsey read from her notes.

"You were right. That's not your best one. Why would I want to pay money to kiss a poster, when I can kiss Ryan?"

"You really feel that way?"

"You better believe it! Oh, stop! Wait!" Blaine giggled, and the phone on her end banged on something.

"Hello. Blaine, are you there?" Lindsey called.

Blaine was laughing when she picked up the phone. "I'm here. Ryan heard what I said and he —" She started to laugh again. "I have to go, Lin. Think up a better idea. Maybe something old-fashioned with boys and girls participating."

"Blaine!"

"I second that motion," Ryan called in the background, just before her friend hung up.

Lindsey went back to staring at the paper, but nothing new came to mind. She sighed and made a large X through the idea. "Blaine's right. Who would pay for that when they could have the real thing? I have to come up with something as wonderful as the real thing that everyone will like. But what?"

Seven

"Squeeze over a tad," Monica said. She and John were the last two to join the group in the big corner booth at Frannie's, Monday after school.

When the meeting was called to order, each person reported on plans for his or her area of responsibility.

"And Mr. Warren said he'd be glad to help with the food, so Blaine and Ryan, you contact Lindsey's dad as soon as you know how much food we'll need. The attendance figures are all in the report from last year, if you need that information." Bill closed his notebook. "Meeting adjourned until next week when we plan our construction schedule."

"Wait," Monica said. "Lindsey didn't report on the kissing booth."

Lindsey started to speak, but Alicia interrupted. "You didn't tell us if Mr. Harley approved all of our ideas, Bill."

"Mr. Harley!" Lindsey said. "When did you see him?"

"This afternoon." Bill riffled the pages of his notebook and didn't look at her.

"And where was I? I thought we were *co*-chairpeople?"

"I didn't ask to see him. He called me in for a quick review of our progress. I didn't think you'd mind."

"So what did he say?" Lindsey could sense the others watching her. It probably wasn't Bill's fault the principal had called only him. Mr. Harley probably didn't understand what co-chairpeople were, either. And maybe the principal had said no to the kissing booth. Then she wouldn't have to come up with an idea if he'd vetoed the idea. She crossed her fingers in her lap.

"Mr. Harley approved almost everything, including the spaghetti eating contest and the dunk tank as long as they were both outside," Bill said.

"What didn't he approve?" John asked.

"Pie throwing — too wasteful and too messy, he said. And he has some reservations about the kissing booth," Bill said. "I assured him it wouldn't be the ordinary, old-fashioned kind of kissing booth, but he wants you to come in and see him about your ideas, Lindsey. He's going to a regional education conference tomorrow, but he'll be back to school next week. Other than that, we're home free. All we have to do is work."

"What kind of reservations does he have about the kissing booth?" Lindsey asked.

Bill looked uncomfortable. "He said, 'No kissing.'"

"That's all?" Ryan asked. "Lindsey can come up with something, I'm sure. No kissing! How can you have a kissing booth with no kissing. That's — that's un-American!"

"Why don't we just cancel the kissing booth?" Alicia asked.

Lindsey was about to agree. "I. . . ." she began.

"That wouldn't be fair to Lindsey," Bill interrupted.

"That's right. She has a couple of plans worked out already. Don't you, Lin?" Blaine said. "You'll convince Mr. Harley."

"I — I guess," Lindsey said weakly.

"That's all the business for today then," said Bill.

"Would anyone like to order a pizza?" Alicia asked.

"I'll go in on one," Ryan said.

"Me, too," said Blaine. "Lindsey?"

She shook her head. "No. I have to get home." And try to do the impossible, she thought — come up with a nonkissing kissing booth. But that had been her idea to start with, hadn't it? She felt confused.

"I'll give you a ride, if you'd like, Lindsey," Bill said. "John, Monica, do you want a ride?"

"Not today," John said. "We have to run over to the library. We have to get some books on biological warfare."

"Oh? Are you planning something?" Ryan asked.

"No. But I think Mr. Shaeffer is," Monica said. "He gave the whole biology class the same assignment. Rather a strange one, don't you think?"

"Not for Mr. Shaeffer," Alicia said. "Last year the topic was gene splicing. Try finding a lot of information on that topic. It's almost top secret."

"Spliced jeans. Isn't that a hazard of over-eating?" Ryan asked.

Everyone groaned.

Even Blaine pointed a thumb down.

"O'Connor, you need a new joke writer," said John, as he and Monica left.

"While you're eating, consider the possibility of selling slices of pizza at the carnival," Bill said as he slid out of the booth.

"What a slave driver!" Alicia complained. "The meeting is over."

"Don't you think about anything except the carnival?" Ryan asked.

"I bet he does." Blaine glanced at Lindsey.

She pretended not to notice. Her friend was turning into an incurable Cupid.

"None of you appreciate the burdens of a co-chairperson," Bill said. "Right, Lindsey?"

"Right," she said. Or the burden of planning a kissing booth where you don't kiss anyone, she thought.

"Lindsey, it looks as if you have a private limousine today," Bill said. "Let's go."

Afternoon traffic sped by on Twelve Mile Road. The sun felt warm on Lindsey's face as she and Bill crossed the parking lot.

"How is the kissing booth coming?" Bill asked as he unlocked the car door. "Was Blaine right? Do you have some plans?"

"Sort of." Lindsey dropped her books in the center of the seat and slid in after them.

"You aren't going to give me any details?" Bill got in on the driver's side.

"None. I'll save them for Mr. Harley when I have *my* private meeting with him."

"Hey, I'm sorry about that. I'll make it up to you. To prove I believe in sharing, will you go shopping with me tomorrow?"

"Shopping for what?" Lindsey asked as the car eased into traffic.

"Lumber, primarily. We have some booths that we reuse every year, but we have to build the platform for the dunk tank and the kissing booth. Also, I'd like to stop by a party store to see what's available that we might be able to use for the fish pond. That's always popular with the little kids. And we need prizes for some of the other booths. Will you go along?"

Lindsey nodded. "All right, providing you don't try to get any more information from me about the kissing booth."

"That's asking a lot, you know. As cochairperson, I'm supposed to know what's going on."

"I can tell you I've already scrapped my first idea."

"Probably Mr. Harley's doing. Well, that's a start. I don't give up easily. Eventually I'll learn your whole plan." His grin was contagious.

Lindsey almost wished she had a definite plan to tell him.

"Here we are," he said as he stopped the car in front of her house a short while later.

"Would you like to come in for a snack?" She'd spoken the words automatically. She used to ask Ross the same question when they came home from school.

"Thanks, but no thanks. I have a lot of homework tonight. See you around school, Lindsey."

"See you. And thanks for the ride, Bill."

He honked the horn before driving away.

"You're smiling," Trina said, opening the door before Lindsey reached the porch.

"Is there anything wrong with that?"

"No. And I know why you're smiling."

"Why?"

"Because Bill drove you home."

"Don't be silly." Lindsey dropped her books near the bottom of the stairs and went to the kitchen. She poured a glass of orange juice.

Trina sat at the kitchen table and watched her. "I'm not silly. I'd be happy if Bill drove me home. He's nice. Right, Piper?"

Piper woofed softly.

"You're both silly. I'm happy because Monday is almost over. No one likes Mondays."

"I don't know why you won't admit that

he's nice," Trina persisted. "I didn't say you loved him."

"Trina, for Pete's sake!"

"But I bet you could if you'd forget about Ross."

"Oh! I don't believe you. Leave me alone. Take Piper for a walk." The heat Lindsey felt wasn't from the spring sun.

"We just came back. Are you going out with Bill this weekend?"

"No, but —"

"But what?"

"Nothing."

"Is he coming over?"

"How did you know?"

"If you aren't going out, he must be coming over."

"Talk sense, Trina."

"I am. By the way, Ross called."

The glass made a loud clink as Lindsey sat it on the counter by the sink. "What did he want?"

"To talk to you. I told him you were with Bill."

"At a meeting, Trina."

"I didn't tell him that."

"Well, you should have."

"Why? You don't like him anymore, do you?"

"No, but —"

"Then it doesn't matter. I told the truth."

"What did he say?"

"He hung up on me."

Lindsey sighed. Trina was right. It

shouldn't matter. Why did it seem to, then?

After changing into old jeans and a beige cotton sweater, Lindsey sat down to work on the kissing booth plans. There had to be some other idea she could use. Kiss, kisses, kissing, she thought, and drew hearts. A kiss for luck. Kisses sweeter than wine. Kisses and roses. Sealed with a kiss. That was a possibility. There were lots of stickers that said sealed with a kiss or SWAK on them. She could hand those out at the kissing booth. But they couldn't charge more than a quarter for them. And how big a market would there be for them? She sighed and dropped her pencil. Where was the right idea? The unique, new-fashioned idea?

The mail flap on the front door banged. A late delivery? she wondered. Lindsey went to see what had come. There was one envelope on the entry hall tile. She picked it up. Her name was written across the front. She recognized the handwriting. Ross.

She opened the door, but there was no sign of him or his car. Forgetting about the problem of the kissing booth, Lindsey ran upstairs. She closed her bedroom door and sat on the edge of her bed. Carefully she slid her finger under the seal on the envelope, then pulled out the single sheet of paper from inside.

Lindsey,

I called, but you weren't home. Forget Bill Stark. Let's go to the Spring Carnival together. Remember last year? I need your answer now. Call me.

Ross

"Just 'Ross,'" said Lindsey, folding the paper. "Not 'Love, Ross.'" His note was as demanding as he was.

Why was she able to think clearly about Ross when he wasn't there, but when she came face to face with him or heard his voice on the phone, she wavered? "I'm not as independent as I think I am," she said, staring at the envelope in her hand. She looked at the phone. Downstairs the doorbell rang. Piper woofed. Lindsey was vaguely aware of the murmur of voices.

"Lin, someone's here to see you," Trina called from downstairs.

Lindsey went to the rail in the hall. "Who is it?" she asked.

"It's me. I have to talk to you, Lindsey." Ruthanne Kramer stood at the bottom of the stairs. She looked upset.

"Sure. Come on up." Lindsey quickly stuffed the envelope in her back pocket as Ruthanne came up to meet her. Had she seen Ross slip it in the mail slot? No, she thought. I didn't even see him. "Come in my room," she said.

Ruthanne looked pretty in a red jumpsuit. She stopped inside the door and looked around. "Where is it?" she asked.

"Where is what?"

"Ross's picture. He said he couldn't get it from you, but I wonder if he even tried."

Lindsey swallowed. "What makes you wonder that?"

"I've seen him looking at you in the hall at school. And I've seen you looking back."

"Not recently," Lindsey said.

Ruthanne seemed not to hear. "And at Frannie's, after we saw you, he was impossible. No fun at all."

"That's not my fault, Ruthanne. Ross and I aren't going together anymore."

"Well, he must think you are, or still wish you were. Let him go, Lindsey. You can't have all the boys at Woodcreek. You have Bill Stark now. I want Ross to like me."

"I don't have Bill Stark. We're on a committee together to plan the Spring Carnival. And I'm not keeping Ross from liking you."

"Then why won't he tell me if we're going to Spring Carnival? It's not that far off. And why wouldn't you give him his picture?" Ruthanne twisted the strap on her purse nervously. "I like him a lot, Lindsey, but he hardly seems to notice me because of you. Are you trying to get him back?"

"No!" Lindsey sat on her bed. "Ross is just — possessive. It's he who doesn't want to let go," she said, conscious of the letter in her back pocket.

"What about the picture?" Ruthanne hadn't moved from inside the doorway. She glared at Lindsey.

"I tried to give it to him."

"Sure." Ruthanne sounded sarcastic.

"Ask him."

"I did." Obviously looking for the photograph of Ross, Ruthanne continued to glance around the room. "What do you mean you tried to give it to him?" she asked.

Lindsey knew if she told Ruthanne the whole story, she'd be hurt. But was she doing her a favor by not telling? She hesitated. Since her break-up with Ross, everything seemed so complicated.

"Let's just say he left without it. But now that you're here —" What was she saying? Could Ruthanne be right? Was she holding on to Ross? Lindsey marched to the closet. She yanked the door open and took out the photograph once more. "You take it with you. Give it to Ross or keep it. I — I don't care."

"Are you sure?" Ruthanne was finally smiling. "He looks so dreamy. Lindsey, I don't blame you for not wanting to let go of him. He tried to tell me it hasn't been easy for you. And believe me, I've tried to understand how you feel, but — " Ruthanne sighed and didn't finish her sentence. "Thanks. I'll tell Ross you gave me the picture."

Ruthanne's words were slowly sinking in. Ross seemed to think she couldn't live without him. Wasn't that what he'd said himself? Well, he was wrong.

"Sorry if I came on too strong," Ruthanne said. "But, well, I really like him. I want him to like me as much."

Lindsey nodded. "I have work to do for the

carnival now, Ruthanne. You'd better leave."
She struggled to keep her voice calm. "Oh,
and tell Ross I said he should take you. I'm
not waiting around to go with him, if he
thought I was."

"I'll tell him." Ruthanne's steps were quick
and light as she hurried out of Lindsey's
room. She clasped Ross's picture to her, every
few steps stopping to look at it. "Thanks,
Lindsey," she called, when she reached the
bottom of the stairs.

Lindsey stood by the upstairs banister,
watching. Maybe she should say thanks to
Ruthanne, but now she felt the same way she
had when she'd first broken up with Ross.
She hoped this was the final good-bye — that
this time the strings had all been broken. She
walked slowly back to her room, where she
tore Ross's note into dozens of little pieces.
They fell like snow into her wastebasket.

"Lin, are you all right?" Trina peered
around the corner of the bedroom door. Her
eyes were wide and serious.

Lindsey nodded.

"I'll set the table for you tonight if you
want."

"That's all right, Trina. I'll do it."

Trina ran to Lindsey and hugged her
quickly. In a minute she was gone again.

"Thanks," Lindsey said softly.

E^{ight}

Later that evening, when she was in bed and thinking about Ruthanne and the happenings of that afternoon, Lindsey got the idea for the kissing booth. Actually Ruthanne hadn't given her the idea — Trina had.

Lindsey switched on her bedside lamp. Propped against her pillow, she jotted some notes. She'd need last year's attendance figures from Bill, and she'd have to talk with her dad. The kissing booth would be great! Even Mr. Harley would agree — she hoped.

The next morning, she spoke with her father. "I can get what you need, honey," he said. "And I think I'll get in line at the carnival."

Lindsey hugged him.

"What happened to you?" Blaine asked when Lindsey dropped into the bus seat beside her.

"Nothing. Why?"

"You look happy."

"I do? Is there something wrong with that?" She smiled.

"You do and of course there's nothing wrong with that. Is there anything you want to tell me?"

"No." Lindsey shook her head and gazed out the window. The lawns were showing a tinge of green and so were the trees. A little warm sun worked wonders.

"Lin, come on. I listen when things are terrible."

Lindsey turned back to Blaine. "I have a great plan for the kissing booth."

"That's all?"

"What do you mean, that's all?" Lindsey frowned. "It hasn't been easy."

"Oh. Well, I thought maybe you and Bill — "

Lindsey shook her head. "Something else did happen, though," she said, suddenly feeling serious again.

"What?"

Lindsey told her about Ruthanne's visit.

"I hope she's happy with him," said Blaine. "Now maybe he'll leave you alone."

"Maybe," Lindsey echoed. But she wasn't sure if she sounded pleased or disappointed.

Bill was waiting at her locker when she entered school. "Are you flexible?" he asked when she approached.

"What do you mean?"

"Can you shop for the carnival a little later today instead of right after school? I have an appointment with my counselor to discuss college. It'll take only an hour."

"Sure. I'll call Trina while I'm waiting for you. She can start dinner tonight."

"I'll meet you here." Bill started away.

"Guess what?" Lindsey said.

He didn't turn back.

I guess he didn't hear me, she thought, as she opened her locker door. Just as well. I really don't want to tell anyone about my plans for the kissing booth — not yet.

Spring showers had dampened the streets by the time school was over, and a gentle rain was still falling when Lindsey and Bill left for their shopping trip.

The old station wagon bumped over the ruts and holes left behind in the lumber company parking lot from the combination of overburdened trucks and heavy winter snows.

"Sorry, I don't have an umbrella," Bill said. "We'll have to make a run for it."

"I don't care. I love the rain." Lindsey zipped her blue jacket and opened the car door. Bill grabbed her hand, and they jumped several puddles on their way toward the huge building that held boards of every length and width.

"Do you know what we'll need?" Lindsey asked as they stepped inside, stopping to wipe their feet on the mat. The building seemed deserted.

"I have a list." Bill patted his shirt pocket. "Let's look in the bargain bin first."

To the right of the door was a box of assorted molding pieces. Bill pulled out two. He handed one to Lindsey.

"Do we need these?" she asked.

"Absolutely." He balanced a three-foot length of molding on his shoulder. "Attenhut! Fall in! Company march!" With exaggerated steps, Bill started marching down the first aisle. "Brrum pum pum. Brrum pum pum," he said, sounding like a drum and marching in time.

"Bill!" Lindsey ran to catch up.

"Whoops! Forgot. We're co-generals. I know, we'll have a parade. See the band behind us? Bomp, bomp, bomp, bomp. Bomp-bomp, bomp-bomp, bomp." He pretended to beat a big drum. Then he held the molding up and pretended it was a trombone. "You don't play an instrument? Well then, get your baton ready. Major and majorette." He tried to twirl the stick of lumber, but dropped it. The clatter of the wood hitting the cement floor seemed to echo in the high-ceilinged metal building.

Lindsey waited for an angry salesman to appear, but no one came.

Bill shook his hand and peered at his finger. "Ouch! I got a sliver."

"Let me see." Lindsey put her stick down. His skin felt warm as he placed his hand in hers. Only his senior class ring held a hint of cold. "I don't see a sliver," she said, and couldn't bring herself to look into his eyes.

"Oh?" He didn't take his hand away, but

leaned forward so that their heads touched. "It was right there. Hmm. I don't see it, either. You must have made it better."

His nearness made her pulse march, a definite band rhythm. Embarrassed and wondering if he could tell, she let go of his hand. "They'll throw us out of here," Lindsey said, bending to pick up the molding.

"No, they won't." He smiled and continued to look at her. "We're customers."

"An army platoon and a marching band?" Lindsey tried to keep her voice light.

"Right." Bill retrieved his molding, too. "Come on. Let's be a parade. You be the leader." He stepped behind her. "Carry that flag up straight. Ready? March."

Lindsey found herself high-stepping down the aisle with Bill behind her counting, "One, two. One, two. Right turn toward the bargain aisle. Hup, two."

She started to laugh. "This is crazy," she said.

"But fun. Life can't always be serious, especially when you have a whole lumber company to yourself. My turn to lead the parade." He marched around her, doing some fancy steps.

Lindsey followed him down the long aisles, inhaling the tangy scent of cut lumber. Rain pattered softly on the metal roof.

"I thought I heard someone out here. May I help you?" An older man with a thin mustache and a pencil tucked behind his left ear intercepted them at the end of one aisle. The tag on his shirt said Quincy.

Bill lowered the piece of molding, and acting as if he frequently marched the aisles of lumber companies, he explained what they needed and why.

"What kind of booths are you building this year?" he asked as he led them toward the back.

"Two new ones — a dunk tank and a kissing booth."

The man smiled and glanced at Lindsey. "Is that going to be your booth, missy? You'll make your boyfriend here jealous."

"I — he —" Lindsey's tongue seemed to be tied in knots. She felt her face burn and knew she was blushing.

"She knows I look good in green," Bill said.

"You should buy all the tickets, son. That's what I'd do," said the salesman, as they stopped in front of the area with the overhead sign marked "Bargains."

"It's not going to be that kind of kissing booth," Lindsey finally managed to say.

"What kind?" Quincy looked puzzled. "How many kinds are there?"

"Bill, don't we have to go to another store yet today?" Lindsey asked.

"Making a mystery of it, huh?" Quincy said. "Guess I'll have to come to your carnival and see about that kissing booth for myself. You don't mind, do you?" he asked Bill, pretending to nudge him.

"We hope you do come, sir," Bill said.

"And kiss your girl?" The salesman chuckled.

Bill glanced at Lindsey. "That's up to her," he said. "She's in charge."

Lindsey said nothing.

They chose lumber from the bargain booth, finding half of what they needed. The salesman helped them get the rest from the regular bins.

"Want this delivered to the school?" he asked.

"Is there a charge?" Lindsey asked.

"Let me check. Maybe we can do you a favor." The salesman hurried away.

"What a character," Bill said. "How many kinds of kissing booths are there anyway?"

Lindsey shook her head. She pretended to be interested in a display of parquet floor squares.

"Aw, come on. You can tell your boyfriend. After all, we've marched the aisles of Franklin Lumber Company together."

Startled, Lindsey turned to look at Bill. His eyes twinkled mischievously. She was rescued from having to respond by Quincy's return.

"The boss says he'll make a donation: free delivery to the school. Do you need anything else? Nails? Tools? Paint?"

"Nails," Bill said.

"You got it." The salesman wrote on his order pad. "Thanks for coming in," he said when they'd paid for the lumber. "See you at the carnival." He winked at Lindsey.

She pretended not to see.

The rain had stopped and slender rays of sun poked from between the clouds.

"Next stop, the party store." Bill backed the car out. "That old guy was getting to you, wasn't he?"

"He was patronizing."

"He was teasing you."

"Well, I hope he doesn't show up at the kissing booth. He'll be disappointed."

"How so?"

"You know what Mr. Harley said."

"Do you mean to tell me you actually have an idea for a kissing booth with no kisses?"

Lindsey hesitated. "Yes — and no."

"That doesn't make sense."

"It will."

"I know — when the booth is set up."

"Couldn't have said it better," Lindsey said.

Bill seemed to be in paradise in the party store. He grabbed two plastic frogs from a box on the shelf. Each frog had a long cord with an air bulb attached. When you squeezed the bulb, the frog jumped. "Rrribit. Rrribit. Rrrace you." He handed one frog to Lindsey, and they propelled the frogs down the aisle. Bill made sound effects, but Lindsey's frog won the race.

"We'll take a dozen of these," Lindsey said. She ran back to get a cart from the line near the door.

"Let's see what else they have." Bill tried the yo-yo's, Superballs, and had Lindsey laughing until she ached at his antics with the disguises: glasses with plastic noses and fuzzy mustaches attached, bloodshot eyeballs, crazy fangs, and masks. He walked down the aisle wearing a droopy handlebar mustache, talking with an exaggerated British accent, and pretending to hold a lorgnette to his eye. She was embarrassed as other shoppers looked at them.

"Bill, be serious," she said.

He bowed. "Quite, my dear," he said, then disappeared down the aisle and returned with a different mustache and a curly wig. "How serious, my dear?" he asked. He lifted her hand to his lips and kissed it.

"Bill, stop it!" This was worse than the lumber store.

"Only if you'll smile."

She gave an exaggerated grin.

"Beautiful!" He put the disguises back, and they finished their shopping.

"I'm glad you can smile," he said as they unloaded their cart of items at the checkout counter.

"What do you mean?" Lindsey asked.

"Since the first carnival meeting, you've been so serious. Bet you have a few permanent frown lines." He ran a finger across her forehead, then playfully down her nose.

Lindsey felt suddenly shy. When he wasn't

in disguise, she didn't know exactly what to say. "You're exaggerating," she muttered.

"We got a lot accomplished," Bill said when they reached her house. "Thanks for going along." He turned to face her.

"Co-chairpeople work together," she said.

Bill looked at her quizzically. "Why so businesslike?"

"One of us has to take this job seriously." Lindsey was vaguely aware of the preachy tone in her voice.

"And you don't think I do?" he asked.

"Marching down the aisle in the lumber store? Trying on disguises at the party store? That's not exactly serious."

"It was lighthearted fun. And it didn't keep us from getting done what we'd set out to do, did it?" Now he both looked and sounded serious. "Why so prickly, Lindsey?"

"You make me sound like a cactus. I'm not prickly."

"Are you sure?"

"Positive. And you're being ridiculous. I have to go in. It's almost time for dinner."

"Sorry if I kept you too late." He opened his door before Lindsey could tell him not to bother. He took her books from her and walked with her to the porch. Trina was waiting there for them.

"Hi, Bill," she said. "My mom said you should come in."

"Oh, she did. Well, I always listen to what moms say."

"Where is she?" Lindsey asked.
way.

"In the kitchen. Follow me." Trina led the

"Hello, Mrs. Warren. You wanted to see me?" Bill asked.

"Yes. Hello. Would you like to stay to dinner tonight? Mr. Warren has a business meeting and won't be home. I've made plenty — nothing fancy, a chicken casserole."

Bill glanced at Lindsey. She didn't say anything. She wanted him to stay and yet she didn't.

"Stay," Trina said. "I want you to."

"In that case, let me call home and let them know. And thanks for the invite, Mrs. Warren."

"You're welcome. Trina, will you set another place? Lindsey, as soon as Bill makes his call, we can eat."

While she washed her hands, Lindsey looked at herself in the mirror. Her eyes looked sparkly and her cheeks were pink. Why didn't she feel that way inside? She hurried to the kitchen.

"Bill, I made dessert just for you," Trina said when they were all seated at the table.

"What kind?" he asked.

"Guess." Trina rested her chin on her hand and gazed at him.

"Stuffed macadamia nuts," Bill guessed.

"What are those?"

"Macadamia nuts? Good stuff," he said.

Trina shook her head. "I didn't make them."

"Not that, huh? Must be stewed dandelion fluff."

"Dandelion fluff! No one eats that." Trina frowned. "You're teasing me like a baby." She sounded hurt.

"Hey, I know you're not a baby," Bill said. "But I was teasing. I tease everyone I like. I'm sorry."

He teases me, Lindsey thought.

"Well, I guess I'm not too mad." Trina smiled again. "Guess some more. What I made is really special, isn't it, Mom?"

Their mother nodded and looked amused.

"I'm all out of guesses. What did you make, Trina?"

"Chocolate brownies."

"My absolute favorite! I can't wait to taste them."

"Honest?" Trina's eyes were wide with pleasure.

"Honest," Bill said. "But first I'd better eat more chicken casserole so your mom won't have her feelings hurt."

"She won't care if you don't eat a lot. She didn't make the chicken casserole just for you."

"Trina!" Lindsey took a helping of green beans and passed them. She had that rubber band feeling again; she wished she could relax.

During dinner, Mrs. Warren asked Bill about the carnival and their shopping trip.

"It sounds as if you're well organized." She stirred her coffee.

"I have a good co-chairperson." Bill glanced at Lindsey. "And with our committee, everything is running smoothly."

"Co-chairperson? That's a funny word," said Trina. "It sounds as if you have to sit together."

Bill laughed. "That's close. It means partners." He winked at Lindsey. "Right, pahdner?"

Lindsey smiled faintly and nodded. He seemed to be charming everyone. Was it all an act, a game? How could you tell when he was serious? Why, now that she thought about it, had he really had a sliver at the lumber company? She curled her fingers in her lap as she remembered holding his hand and the sensation of his head next to hers. It probably meant nothing, she told herself.

"Can't you tell me about the carnival?" Trina asked.

"Can we?" Bill raised his eyebrows. "The publicity goes out next week. How about it, co-chairperson?"

"I don't care," Lindsey said.

"Let's see." Bill told about the games, pet beauty contest, and booths. "And your sister is going to run the kissing booth."

"Lindsey! Why didn't you tell me?" Trina asked.

"I'm working out the plan."

"What's it going to be like?" Trina's eyes were huge with anticipation.

"That's a surprise."

"Top secret," Bill said, putting a finger to his lips. "No one knows."

"I bet you do," Trina said.

"No. Not even me."

"Bill, would you like more casserole?" Lindsey's mother passed the dish.

"Thanks, but I'd better save room for brownies, Mrs. Warren."

"I'll get them now." Trina jumped up from the table. "I'm going to enter Piper in the beauty contest," she said.

"Good idea," Bill said.

On hearing his name, Piper barked and came from under the table, where he'd been begging handouts.

"No brownies for you, Piper," Trina said. "You have to stay skinny for the contest."

When the meal was over and Bill had praised the brownies and the dinner, he helped clear the table. "Thanks again for asking me, Mrs. Warren," he said.

"Come again." She smiled.

"I'd like that."

Lindsey walked with him to the door.

"You have a nice family," Bill said.

"Thank you. The Warrens like you, too."

"All of them?" He didn't give her time to answer, but jumped from the porch and ran down the walk.

Piper barked and raced after him.

"Piper, come back," Lindsey called. Bill bent to pet the dog, then pointed to the house. Piper came slowly up the walk, stopping once to look back. Trina, her parents, even the dog seemed to like Bill, Lindsey thought. She blocked out her own feelings as she returned to the kitchen to help with the dishes.

"He's a nice boy," her mother said, as she rinsed plates and handed them to Lindsey to put in the dishwasher.

"I want to know if he's going to be in the kissing booth," Trina said. "If he is, I'm going to buy bunches of tickets."

Lindsey barely caught the plate that slipped from her fingers. "Trina! Don't you dare!"

"Why? Are you jealous?" Trina struck a model's pose.

"Don't be ridiculous."

"You like him. But if you don't, he could be my boyfriend, because I think he's really cute. Don't you think so, Mom?"

"Trina, shut up!" Lindsey shouted. "You sound stupid!"

"I don't! Mom, she called me stupid!"

"Girls, that's enough," said their mother. "Let's get this kitchen cleaned up. Trina, get the broom and sweep the floor."

As Lindsey ran the wet sponge across the countertop, she thought about Bill. He'd be back again Saturday. They had to make the posters for the Carnival. She could imagine what crazy ideas he'd have for those. She smiled and almost laughed as she recalled his antics at the stores. Then there was dinner. Trina had a crush on him, that was obvious.

He'd charmed the whole family — almost. He was certainly nothing like Ross. Ross had never talked much with anyone but Lindsey when he came to her house. But after Ross, she wasn't taking any chances. No more boys for a while. Lindsey sighed and finished her job.

N_ine_

During the rest of the week there were hurried meetings of the carnival committee during lunch in the cafeteria. Everyone was working feverishly to organize the areas in their charge. Each was eager to report on the latest progress to any willing ear.

Suddenly Saturday came. Several times during the day Lindsey picked up the telephone to call Blaine and discuss her tumultuous feelings about Bill. But each time she didn't complete the dialing and let the receiver drop back in place. How can I talk about something I can't even explain? she wondered. And there was always the memory of Ross in the back of her mind. She'd heard that sometimes girls fall in love on the rebound after breaking up with an old boyfriend. Could that be what was happening?

Wrapped in her old robe and still feeling dampish from her shower, Lindsey stared into her dresser mirror and noticed how flushed her face looked. "Falling in love with Bill? I couldn't be," she said to her image. And yet. . . .

She shook the thought from her head like so many cobwebs that shouldn't be there. A silly idea, she was sure, even though Blaine would be delighted that it had even occurred to her.

Lindsey turned to get dressed. She put on her newest pale blue and white cotton jeans and a matching blue top, then pulled a white net vest over her head. She sat on the edge of her bed and sighed. Her stomach was churning as if this were to be a special date with a special boy tonight, rather than a business meeting with Bill to make carnival posters.

"What time is he coming?" Trina, always energy in motion, skipped into the room and plopped down beside Lindsey.

"Seven."

"I can't wait."

"Trina, please don't bother Bill when he's here."

"I never bother him. He likes me. And I like him." Trina went to the dresser. She picked up a tube of pink lipstick. "How do you think I'd look in this color?" she asked.

"You know Mom says you can't wear lipstick yet."

"Kelly's mother lets her for special occasions."

"This isn't a special occasion."

"Then why are you so dressed up?"

"I'm not." Lindsey went to stand beside her sister and picked up her hairbrush.

"Isn't that your new outfit?"

"Yes. But I have to wear it sometime."

"And sometime is when Bill is coming over."

"Trina, put the lipstick down and stop it."

"Stop what? You get all prickly when I mention his name. How come?"

Bill had called her the same thing. Lindsey sighed. "We have work to do on the carnival posters," she said, avoiding the question.

"So? I can help. Art is one of my good subjects. If you don't like him, you won't care about being alone with him, so you won't mind if I help, will you?"

Lindsey felt Trina watching her. Her stomach knotted, and she wished that Trina was going to Kelly's house for the evening. "If Bill says it's okay, why should I mind?"

Trina looked knowing, then shrugged. "No reason." She touched her lips with a hint of Lindsey's lipstick, then hurried from the room.

Lindsey put on coral lipstick, then dabbed cologne on her wrists, behind her ears, and on her throat. I shouldn't mind at all, she thought. Why do I?

The door bell rang, and she jumped. One more quick look at her hair, then she started down the stairs. Trina was ahead of her and opened the door. Piper bounded from the family room, excited at Bill's arrival, as usual.

He looked up to see Lindsey coming down the stairs. "Blue is just as nice as pink," he said as she reached the bottom step.

"Thanks." For some reason she felt embarrassed by his compliment. "I've set up the posterboard and felt tip pens in the family room. Come this way, Bill."

"May I help? Please?" Trina begged.

Bill looked at Lindsey, but she looked away.

"Sure. Why not?" he asked. "We'll have a poster party."

"Mom and Dad went to the movies," said Trina. "I'm the chaperone tonight."

"Oh, really? Do you think I need one?" Bill asked as they entered the pine-paneled room with the long stone fireplace. Piper trailed behind and settled on his favorite rug.

"I'm not sure," Trina said. "Does he, Lindsey?"

Lindsey pretended not to hear her sister. She hurried toward the Ping-Pong table, where she'd set out the art materials.

"Lindsey doesn't know," Bill said. "Maybe you should stick around and find out."

"Okay!" Trina bounced along beside him, casting admiring glances in his direction.

"Everything is set up," Lindsey said, wishing she didn't sound so formal. "Are you ready to work?"

His green eyes seemed to twinkle as she looked at him. "Any time you are, co-chairperson."

Trina sat at the end of the table, leaving

the side-by-side chairs for Lindsey and Bill.

"How many posters will we need?" Lindsey asked, keeping busy by arranging the felt tip pens in a row.

"Three for each floor, one for the gym, at least a dozen to tack up around town, maybe more. Let's make as many as we can."

They cut the posterboard into smaller squares, then got to work. Lindsey tried to concentrate on drawing balloons.

"Hey, if you're going to sit there, get a pen and some paper and draw, Trina," Bill said, pushing supplies in her direction.

"I can help? All right! What should I draw?"

"Piper," said Bill. "Don't you think that's a good idea, Lindsey?"

Lindsey nodded.

"I'm going to put the stereo on first." Trina hopped up from her chair and went to the corner of the room. Moments later rock music blared from the speakers. She danced back to the table.

Lindsey wished she could be as relaxed as her sister seemed to be. She looked up at Bill. He was bent over his poster, a stray curl falling haphazardly across his forehead, which was creased with a slight frown of concentration. Tonight he wore his green sweater and old jeans. The gold medallion that he wore at his neck swung forward while he worked. As she watched him sketch a dunk tank complete with waves and splashing water, Lindsey recalled how it felt to hold his hand. She shook her head and forced herself to go back to work.

"How does Piper look?" Trina asked after she'd been working for a while.

"Good," Lindsey said. Her sister really did have artistic talent.

"Who is that in the dunk tank?" asked Lindsey, leaning toward Bill. She was close enough to smell the faint scent of his aftershave.

"Mr. H. If I can make this flattering enough, maybe this hint will help."

"Good luck."

He looked at her poster, a group of multicolored balloons in one corner with the information printed in block letters.

"Try outlining your letters in black," he said. "Here, look." He reached over, picked up the black pen, and put a line around the W in Woodcreek. Then he handed the pen to her.

Their fingers brushed and for a second it seemed as if he didn't want to let go. "That looks good," Lindsey said. "I'll do the others."

"I'm going to make some popcorn," Trina said. "Want some?"

"Sounds great." Bill added a few additional strokes to the picture he was drawing. "There." He pushed that poster across the table and took another sheet of posterboard.

They worked quietly, Lindsey wishing she could think of something to say and finding it hard to concentrate. This is silly, she thought. Suddenly I'm acting as if there's something special between Bill and me, and there's nothing.

She started on another poster.

Trina came back with popcorn and drinks. She chattered and drew several posters. Bill answered back, while Lindsey worked quietly and continued to remind herself that they were only co-chairpeople and this was business.

At ten, Bill stretched his arms and yawned. "I've drawn all I can," he said. "Let's count how many posters we have. Six, eleven, fourteen. That will probably be enough. I might see if we can run some fliers on the copy machine at school."

"Do you have to go home now?" Trina asked, yawning, too.

"In a while."

"Shouldn't you go to bed, Trina?" Lindsey asked.

Trina wrinkled her nose. "It's Saturday."

"And it's after ten."

"But how can I chaperone from upstairs?"

"Don't worry. I'll be a perfect gentleman," Bill promised, tickling her with one of her braids.

Trina smiled, then yawned again. "Okay. Goodnight."

"Thanks for helping," Lindsey said.

"Yes, thanks," Bill echoed.

"You're welcome." Trina called Piper, who had been sleeping on the rug in front of the fireplace, then they headed upstairs.

"One big project out of the way," Bill said.

"The carnival is going to happen, I think."

Lindsey nodded.

"You've been quiet tonight." He capped several pens and gathered the rest of the posterboard into a pile.

"I guess I didn't have a lot to say." Lindsey didn't look at him, but pretended to be busy studying the last of the posters they'd completed.

"Mmm. Sometimes quiet is nice — relaxing." He stood up. "I'd better get home. Do you want me to take the posters?"

"Since I take the bus to school, I guess you'd better. I'll help you carry them to the car." Lindsey gathered half the posters, and they walked toward the door.

The air outside felt warm and damp. The scent of rain was in the air. The ratchety noise of frogs was surrounded by the chorus of night insects celebrating a mild spring evening.

They put the posters in the back of the old station wagon.

"I'll walk you back to the door," Bill said.

"You don't have to." Lindsey started across the lawn to the house. The whole evening had been terrible. She'd felt awkward and ill at ease and wanted to get back inside. But the grass was already damp with dew and in her hurry her feet slid from beneath her. Ungracefully she hit the ground, landing on her side before strong arms helped her up.

"I was hoping you'd fall for me," Bill said as he steadied her.

"How can you make a joke?" she asked, looking down at her new pants. Even in the pale glow of the porch light she could see that there was a green and brown stain across the blue. Tears welled behind her eyes. Absolutely nothing had gone right tonight.

"Hey, I'm sorry." Bill turned her to face him and kept his hands on her shoulders. "That was mean," he said, slipping one hand beneath her chin and easing her head back so she had to look up at him. "I shouldn't have teased you."

Lindsey stared into his eyes, serious in a way she'd never seen Bill serious before.

"Lindsey," he said.

The sounds of a car pulling into the drive next to Bill's car made her jump back from him.

"We're home, kids. Did you get your posters finished?" Her mother's cheerful voice followed the slam of a car door.

"Yes," Lindsey said, as she and Bill stepped farther apart.

"Well, I'd better get home," Bill said. "Goodnight, Mr. and Mrs. Warren. Goodnight, Lindsey."

"Goodnight," she said, feeling suddenly chilled by the damp night air.

"Goodnight, Bill," her parents called.

As they reached the porch, the headlights from Bill's car swept across the front of the house. Then she heard the roar of the motor as he drove away.

"What happened to your pants, dear?" her mother asked, as they stepped inside.

Lindsey looked down. The spot was as bad as she'd expected. "I slipped on the lawn," she said. "I hope I can get the stain out."

"Take care of it right away," her mother said as Lindsey's father closed and locked the door behind them.

In the laundry room, Lindsey sprayed stain remover on the grass stain. Memories of the evening floated in and out of her mind. She sighed as she dropped her pants into the washer and pulled the knob to start the water flowing. She wondered if Bill would look at her again Monday the way he had on the lawn tonight. Monday, she thought. Monday she had to see Mr. Harley about the kissing booth. Suddenly she wished she'd been willing to have a real kissing booth. There were some old-fashioned ideas that shouldn't be given up in a struggle for independence and kissing was one of them. But it was too late now. Maybe too late for everything. Lindsey sighed again and leaned on the washer.

Ten

"Mr. Harley gave his permission!" Lindsey broke the news at the final planning meeting for the spring carnival.

"Now will you tell us what the kissing booth is going to be like?" Alicia reached for a french fry off the dish in the center of the table. Frannie's french fries were the best — long, thin, hot, and salty.

"No. But I do want to know if I can choose my own workers or is there a list of volunteers I should use?"

"Lindsey, that's not fair," Monica complained. "You know all about the rest of the carnival plans."

"The kissing booth has to be a surprise. If everyone knows, it won't work." She still couldn't believe how easy it had been to convince Mr. Harley that her idea would work. He'd even been enthusiastic.

"To answer your question," Bill said, "you

can choose whichever workers you want, Lindsey. Service Club has open, automatic membership."

"I still think we should be in on Lindsey's plans," Monica grumbled.

"I second that," John added.

Lindsey shook her head. "You'll find out. . . ."

". . . when we have the carnival," they all finished.

"That booth had better be good." Alicia pushed the plate of french fries across the table.

"It will be." Lindsey hoped she sounded convincing.

"We love your posters," Ryan said. "If the kissing booth is as good as those, it will be a smashing success."

"Smashing success? Where did you get that phrase?" John asked.

"From some old movie, no doubt." Ryan grinned.

"No doubt." John scooped the last of the french fries from the plate.

"We were talking about the posters," Blaine said. "I especially like the one with the dunk tank. The guy in the water looks like Mr. Harley."

"You didn't by any chance talk him into volunteering?" John asked.

"Not yet," Bill said.

"But we keep hinting," Lindsey said. She'd even been brave enough to mention it when she'd seen him. Mr. Harley had smiled and said he'd think about it.

"Let's get on with business. Friday after school construction crews will meet in the school parking lot." Bill handed slips of paper to everyone. "I've split up the phone calls, so one person doesn't have to make them all. Ask the volunteers to bring hammers. We'll have the rest of the tools here. Mr. Kilgore from woodshop has offered to supervise, as usual."

"My dad will help, too," Alicia said.

"And mine," Ryan said.

"All help graciously accepted." Bill closed his notebook. "That's it. The carnival is planned. Now we put the pieces together and hope it's a *smashing* success, as Ryan so aptly put it." He slid out of the booth and put on his jacket. "It's raining again. Does anyone want a ride home?"

Everyone accepted his offer this time.

"Lindsey, I'll drop you off last. There are a few details we have to go over regarding the schedule."

She nodded. Today he was all business again. The look in his eyes had been all in her imagination Saturday night, she decided. Just as well. No more boys. That had been her decision and there was no reason to change it. It was time to get rid of fickle thoughts that tempted to sway her from her common sense course.

"The schedule? That's a likely excuse, Bill." John laughed as he put his arm around

Monica. They walked across the parking lot. "What he really means, Lindsey, is that he wants you to sit in front and have a few minutes alone together after he gets rid of the rest of us." He winked at her and hugged Monica.

Lindsey waited for Bill to deny what John said, but he didn't comment at all. Today at school, Bill had been his usual friendly self, but he'd done nothing nor said a word that would indicate he was especially interested in her. Bill Stark simply wasn't serious. And that was fine; it was best, she told herself.

"I've figured it out," Ryan suddenly announced.

"What?" Alicia and Blaine asked together.

"The kissing booth."

"No you haven't," Lindsey said, wondering if he could have, yet glad that someone had changed the subject away from her and Bill. Lately, everyone seemed to be pushing her toward him.

"What's your theory, Ryan?" Monica asked.

"Lindsey and Bill are going to kiss and charge admission for everyone to watch."

"We are not!" Lindsey exclaimed. "We — Bill, tell them we aren't." She wished she didn't blush. They'd get the wrong idea.

"You just did that with enough emphasis to convince anyone," he said. He smiled but there was something in his voice that sounded different than usual. Probably he's tired, she thought. The carnival had taken a lot of planning; they'd been working hard.

They climbed into the station wagon. Lindsey did sit in front with Alicia, while Blaine and Ryan, Monica and John squeezed into the back seat. Bill was unusually silent as he made the rounds to drop off the others. Finally only Lindsey was left. As soon as Alicia was gone, she moved toward the door. The windshield wipers swished back and forth and Lindsey watched them rather than talk.

Bill turned onto the first street of the small subdivision where Lindsey lived. Rather than being laid out like crisscrossed railroad tracks, the streets wound in random patterns, giving a feeling of country rather than city. Bill drove past Foxtail Lane, Lindsey's street.

"You missed the turn," she said.

"No, I didn't. I want to ask you something." Bill turned on Willow Way Circle and stopped opposite the pond. The willow trees that grew around the bank looked coated with green where new leaves were pushing out from the bowing branches. The rain fell in gentle, large drops that dimpled the water.

"Oh, look! Ducks," Lindsey said.

For a few minutes, they watched the birds swim in a line across the water, sending out a v-shaped trail behind them. She was conscious of Bill only a few inches from her. His arm rested on the back of the seat; if he moved, his arm would rest on her shoulders. She willed herself not to think about that.

"Do you live near here?" Lindsey asked, realizing that she didn't know much about Bill at all.

"Closer to Thirteen Mile Road."

She nodded and searched for something else to say. "You'll graduate this year."

"That's right. Lindsey —" The way he said her name reminded her of Saturday night.

"What are you going to do after?" Lindsey blurted out. She avoided looking at him and continued to watch the ducks.

Bill sighed. "I'm going to Wayne State. I want to be a teacher."

Lindsey was startled. "A teacher?" Now she turned to face him. "Ross always said that teachers are — I mean, I don't know anyone who wants to be a teacher, except you. Are your parents teachers?"

"No. My mother died when I was in junior high. My aunt lives with us. My father's a pharmacist at Henry Ford Medical Center. Anything else you want to know?" He sounded impatient. "Does Ross have an opinion about any of those things?"

"No." Lindsey looked at her hands. Why had she mentioned Ross? She hadn't thought about him for days.

Bill started the car.

She looked at him. "What did you want to ask me? If it's about the kissing booth —"

"It isn't. But this is the wrong time. And I think I know the answer, anyway. I have to get home."

"But —"

"It will wait." As he'd done at the party store, he ran his finger down her forehead then gently tapped the tip of her nose. He put the car in gear.

"If it's important —" Lindsey felt like a little kid saying tell me, tell me. And yet she wasn't sure she wanted to know, either.

"It's too important to rush. I misjudged — my timing. Don't worry about it." He drove the car around the cul-de-sac.

The windshield wipers seemed to say "too bad, too bad" as they beat back and forth. Lindsey felt strangely empty and disappointed. What had he been planning to say? she wondered.

"Do you want to come in?" she asked when he stopped in front of her house.

Bill smiled, but again there was something different about his smile, something about the look in his eyes. They seemed sad. "No. I really do have to get home, Lindsey. I'll see you tomorrow."

"Thanks for the ride," she said, as she opened the door.

"You're welcome."

She slammed the door and ran up the walk. His car was gone before she reached the porch. Lindsey frowned. Was something wrong? she wondered. Had she done something? Was he angry because she refused to tell him about the kissing booth? Maybe that was it. Well, he'd find out soon — they'd all find out. Or was it that she'd asked him questions about himself? But why should that bother him? Or was it her reaction when he said he wanted to be a teacher? At least she hadn't told him what Ross had said about teachers. It wasn't very complimentary. She didn't know why she'd mentioned Ross at all. Maybe it was nothing. Maybe Bill was just late getting home. Maybe she was imagining things again. That was probably more likely, she thought, as she entered the house.

There was a note taped to the refrigerator saying that her mother had to work late on some party arrangements for the florist. Trina was at her friend Kelly's. "Your dad will be late, too. Go ahead and eat without us," Lindsey read. "Love, Mom. P.S. Let Piper out for a few minutes, please."

Piper was happy to see her but he wasn't thrilled about going out in the rain and returned as quickly as possible. He followed Lindsey upstairs and settled near the heat vent.

"I have a lot to do, Piper," she said. Talking to him made the house seem less empty.

First, Lindsey phoned her selected workers, chosen carefully, especially for their ability to keep secrets. She called a meeting for after school the next day. Next, she called the list of people she'd been given for the construction work on Friday, giving them the directions that Bill had requested.

After taking time out to change her clothes, Lindsey pulled the large posterboard from under her bed and took her marking pens from the drawer in her bedside table. Piper snored nearby. She drew a red heart. In the center she carefully lettered the words:

KISSES FOR SALE
Buy kisses!
Get a free hug!
Donation: $1.00

"I hope they'll pay a dollar," she said, as she carefully outlined the letters. But the money was for a good cause. The Spring Carnival supported such extras as field trips, sports uniforms, assemblies, and the music program. The more money they raised, the better the school was.

"Lindsey, are you home?" Trina slammed the front door.

Piper was immediately alert and on his feet. He woofed and scampered toward the bedroom door. Quickly Lindsey capped her pen and pushed the poster under her bed. "I'm in my room," she called.

Trina came up the stairs, her feet pounding as if she was running. "Look what Kelly and I made." She held up what looked like baby clothes. There was a pair of pants and a shirt that said Woodcreek on the front.

"Who are they for?" Lindsey asked.

"Guess." Trina turned the pants around. "There's a hole in the back."

"For the tail," she said.

"Tail?" Lindsey pointed at Piper.

Trina smiled and nodded. "This is Piper's outfit for the beauty contest."

"They're cute, Trina, but will he wear them?" Lindsey got up and examined the clothes.

"We're going to practice, so he's used to them by the carnival. Also, we're making a hat." She looked down at Piper, who sat patiently with droopy ears and sad eyes, waiting to be petted.

"What kind?"

"We think a sailor hat, but we aren't sure. Isn't Mom home yet?"

"No. She must be working on a big party."

"I guess. Will Dad be here for dinner?"

"Not on time. We'd better fix something for ourselves."

"Make scrambled eggs with cheese. I love that." Trina sat on the floor and hugged the dog. "Piper does, too, don't you, Piper?"

"All right. Your turn to set the table."

"I know. I'll be right there. Piper, look what I have for you." Trina tried to slip the shirt over his head, but he ducked out of her way.

Lindsey went downstairs to start dinner. Rain spattered against the kitchen windows. Her reflection looked back at her from the glass. Her conversation with Bill nagged at her, making her feel unsettled. Why hadn't he asked her what he'd been going to ask? she wondered. Why couldn't she keep him out of her mind? It was no use, she thought as she tried to remember everything they'd said by the pond.

"Lindsey!"

"Hmm?" She turned around.

"I've called you three or four times. Look at Piper."

Piper's tail wasn't wagging where it poked through the hole in the pants he wore. He looked as sad as a basset hound could look.

Lindsey smiled. "I don't think he likes his new outfit."

"I know, but he isn't tearing it apart, either. That's a good sign. I think he'll have to wear the shirt backward, don't you? You can't see the writing on his stomach."

Lindsey nodded and petted Piper. "You'll be beautiful," she said.

Piper whined and rubbed against her.

They finished making dinner and ate.

The spring shower turned into a storm as the hour grew late. Shortly after eight, their mother stamped her feet inside the door and propped her umbrella to dry.

"Did you eat?" Lindsey asked.

"We sent out for Chinese food. Your dad's not here yet?"

Lindsey shook her head.

"The driving is bad." Her mother looked worried.

An hour later their father pulled his car into the drive. Everyone jumped up at the slam of his door.

"Duck weather," he said, brushing the water from his coat.

Duck weather, Lindsey thought. She remembered ducks swimming in straight lines across a rain dimpled pond and herself asking question after question which Bill patiently answered.

In bed that night she tossed and turned. What was he going to ask her? If it was important, he'll probably ask me tomorrow, she thought, as she struggled to settle her mind and get to sleep. But she kept remembering how he looked and how he sounded. Finally she sat up in her bed and hugged her knees. Rain splashed against the windows, and the wind seemed to cry to come inside. Lindsey gave up trying to block out thoughts of Bill. Resting her head on her knees, she replayed every minute they'd been together since the first meeting of the carnival committee. And then she knew what had been different about Bill today. The spark had been missing from Stark the Spark. But why?

$E\underline{leven}$

The meeting of the kissing booth committee went smoothly the next day. Each person who huddled in a circle in the back of the home economics room was sworn to secrecy.

"Tom, if you'll take charge of scheduling," Lindsey said, "no one will have to spend too much time at the booth. That way everyone has a chance to enjoy the carnival."

"This is going to be a riot," said Grace Truit, a sophomore. "What if someone gets angry?"

"They're getting their money's worth," said Joe Livingston, "and most people are good sports."

"Remember, don't give the plan away," Lindsey warned.

"No one knows about it?" asked Jennifer Allen, a junior, who worked at Frannie's.

"No one," said Lindsey, "except Mr. Harley and now you."

"How about Ross Jordani?" Tom asked.

"She's not dating him anymore," said Grace.

"Oh yeah?" Tom looked surprised.

"Isn't it Bill Stark now?" asked Jennifer.

"What is this — a gossip group?" Lindsey asked. "I'm not dating anyone, if you must know. I've been too busy working on the carnival."

"With Bill," said Keith Goldman. "But I don't hear him complaining."

Lindsey felt her face growing warm. This is ridiculous, she thought. "He will be, if we don't get this carnival put together."

"When do we meet again?" asked David Williams.

"Friday, right after school, to assemble our packages," Lindsey said.

"Can I give out a real kiss if I want?" Sherry asked.

"I don't want to know about it if you do," Lindsey said. "Mr. Harley said no."

"My lips are sealed," said Sherry.

"Hey, that's a good motto for our group," Joe said.

They all laughed.

On Friday, Lindsey went from her meeting with the "lips are sealed" group, to the parking lot where the construction was being organized. Everyone scattered to their assigned areas.

Lindsey had agreed Bill would handle this part of the carnival because she had her booth to organize. Now, as she and Blaine pounded nails under Mr. Kilgore's expert direction, building the kissing booth, she wished she'd asked to share the assignment with him. They'd had little time to talk all week. She thought of him constantly and missed him.

When dinner break was over, the last of the pizza gone, and only one case of soft drinks left, it was time to paint. Spotlights shone across the concrete parking lot. The sounds of hammers and saws still echoed on the Woodcreek High school grounds. The sky had a smattering of clouds, which scudded rapidly across the face of the moon. A stiff breeze was drying the last of the rain that had fallen on and off during the week.

"We might be lucky," Bill said, as he made the rounds, checking to be sure that every booth had someone there to see it was properly assembled.

"Bill, we need a longer hose to fill the pool," John called. "I'm going to drive over to Monica's to borrow theirs. She's going with me."

"Remember to come back," Ryan called.

"We won't forget." Monica popped from behind a booth where she'd been pinning up crepe paper streamers.

Lindsey and Blaine were busy with paint brushes and red paint.

"How will this kissing booth work again?" Blaine asked.

Lindsey smiled and shook her head. "Nice try," she said. "I'll give you a hint: the right side will be boys and the left side girls."

"But no kissing." Blaine frowned. "This has to be the best kept secret at Woodcreek."

"Lindsey, will you have enough paint?" Bill stopped by, a clipboard in his hand.

"Plenty. We'll be ready," she said. "My volunteers are all set, too." She smiled and hoped he'd notice.

"Good." He made a notation and moved off without another glance her way.

Lindsey watched him.

"Ahem. I said, ahem!"

Lindsey jumped.

Blaine stuck out her tennis shoe. It was splotched with a fat blob of red paint. "You're dripping," she said.

"Oh, sorry." Lindsey tried to wipe the paint off with a rag, but that made it worse.

Blaine shook her head. "Put one on the other foot so they match," she said.

Lindsey obliged.

"Were you too busy watching Bill to pay attention to your painting?"

"No. Why would I watch him?" Lindsey vigorously stirred the paint.

"Want a couple guesses?"

"No."

"You know what they'd be. You've been looking for him all week — in the halls, in the cafeteria, after school. What's going on?"

"Nothing. Nothing's going on."

"I see." Blaine dabbed paint along the counter of the booth. "But you're working on something going on soon?"

"I'm working on painting this booth and making this carnival a success — that's all."

Blaine smiled and started to hum to herself. "At least you finally let go of Ross," she said softly.

Lindsey brushed the paint on in long, vigorous strokes. That was true, she thought, not bothering to answer Blaine. She hadn't actually thought about Ross since she'd mentioned him to Bill. And she never looked for him in the halls at school anymore. Blaine was right about her looking for Bill, though she wouldn't admit it.

She remembered the day they went shopping — the fun they'd had, even though he'd embarrassed her. And the dinner at her house. And making the posters together. But things seemed different lately. Ever since Bill had parked near the duck pond, he seemed to be avoiding her. He was always too busy to talk, too busy to stop, too busy. . . .

Maybe it's me, she thought. Maybe I've been too independent. Maybe he wants a shadow, too, just like Ross. Lindsey sighed. What was she thinking about Bill for anyway? She was going to give up boys — remember? But she couldn't help looking across the yard where he was talking to Mr. O'Connor and Mr. Kilgore. She couldn't help her feelings.

"You're out of paint, Lindsey." Ryan looked amused as he passed by. "Better keep her from thinking ahead to that great kissing booth, Blaine. You won't get your work done."

"And you won't get yours done, either," Lindsey called after him, "if you keep snoopervising."

"You have been brushing that same spot for the last five minutes." Blaine smiled.

"I'm just doing a thorough job," Lindsey said, but she guessed that her face probably looked as red as the paint. Why had she taken up blushing so much lately? With determination, Lindsey forced herself to concentrate on her work. Keeping busy was always the answer, she told herself. It worked with Ross; it would work with Bill. She'd keep him out of her mind. She was starting to believe the rumors everyone had repeated to her about herself and Bill, that was the trouble. No more. Busy, busy, busy, she said to herself as she dabbed the paint in the corners.

Blaine put her brush down and glanced at her watch. "Oh, oh. We'd better hurry. I have to have the car home before eight and it's twenty to already. My mom has her bowling league tonight."

"You go ahead," Lindsey said. "I'll finish up here."

"I've got time to do this panel over the top. That's the last part. Will this paint dry by tomorrow?" Blaine asked.

"It better. With the wind, it probably will." Lindsey started on the left side of the board and Blaine on the right. They met in the middle.

"Finished!" Blaine said. "Looks great!"

Lindsey stepped back. "I wonder if we'll be able to move this inside the gym tonight?"

"Ask Bill. Here he comes."

"If you two are through with painting here, John could use some help with the dunk platform," he said.

"I can't. I have to get the car home," Blaine said.

"Do you have to leave, too, Lindsey?" Bill asked.

"She doesn't have to if she can get a ride with someone else," Blaine said.

"I'll call my mom or dad," Lindsey said.

"I can take you home, Lindsey," Bill offered, "if you want me to."

"All right, I'd — " She was interrupted by Alicia calling Bill.

"Fine. It's all arranged," he said as he hurried away.

"Wasn't that easy?" Blaine asked. "Your grandmother would say we just killed two birds with one stone."

"He's always giving people rides. I'll probably be one of a dozen," Lindsey said.

"And suddenly it matters."

"I — yes, it matters," Lindsey admitted.

"Good. An independent girl needs an independent guy. If you have time, call me when you get home." Blaine ran across the parking lot toward her car.

Lindsey capped the paint cans and went to rinse the brushes off. It might matter to me, she thought, but I don't think it matters to

Bill. I'm just a co-chairperson, that's all. How confused she felt. All this time she'd been claiming that's all she was, all she wanted to be. When had that all changed? She wasn't sure.

The kissing booth was the last one brought into the gym. The paint was dry, the curtains were hung on the right and left of the counter, the signs were up.

"You're giving hugs free?" Bill asked as he came by to inspect her booth.

Lindsey nodded, feeling shy with him.

"But there'll be no kisses."

"Oh, there will be, but —" Lindsey caught herself. "But you'll have to find out tomorrow."

He looked at her and nodded. "I might just do that." Then he was flipping papers on the clipboard. "We can leave in about fifteen minutes. I think we have everything as ready as it can be. One more round of booths."

"I'll be waiting," Lindsey said.

Almost everyone commented on her sign, trying to get her to explain how she could say Kisses For Sale and not sell any kisses. She smiled and told them to find out tomorrow. "Only a dollar," she said. "For a good cause."

Bill and Lindsey walked with Mr. Kilgore out of the gym. The lights were out.

"You kids have outdone yourselves this year," the shop teacher said. "A professional job, this carnival."

"Thanks," Bill said, "for the compliment and especially for helping us tonight."

"Did I hear right that Mike Harley has volunteered to be dunked?" the teacher asked.

"Um —" Bill glanced at Lindsey. "That was supposed to be top secret."

"He did?" Lindsey asked. "When?"

"Just this morning," Bill said. "Not a word to anyone."

"You've kept it a secret," she said.

"We all have our secrets," Bill said. "Like the kissing booth."

"Oh yes. The kissing booth," Mr. Kilgore said. "Now, Mike wouldn't tell us about that. He only said that no one would be critical."

"Lindsey's done a great job with it," Bill said.

She heard the praise in his voice and smiled at him. When he smiled back, it gave her a warm feeling inside.

They parted at the station wagon, Mr. Kilgore going to his Honda.

"Will you be glad when tomorrow is over?" Lindsey asked as Bill started the car.

"Yes and no. It's been hard work, but fun — especially working with you, Lindsey."

"I think so, too, Bill. I haven't seen much of you this week."

"Been busy. You know how it is. Seniors have a lot of papers and college tests to take."

"Mm." Lindsey nodded. This was like the night they made posters. She felt awkward trying to make conversation. She didn't want to start asking questions the way she had at the pond, yet there was a lot she wanted to know — especially what he really thought of her and what that unasked question was.

They were at her house much too soon. Bill walked her to the porch. "See you in the morning. I can pick you up if you want," he said.

"Okay. I'd like that. Please."

"So would I." He held her hand. For a minute, she thought he was going to say more. But he squeezed her hand, let go, and turned back to the walk. "I'll be here around eight," he called.

Lindsey waved and watched until his car was too far away to see.

When she opened the door, she almost knocked Trina over. "What were you doing?"

"Watching you," Trina said, looking guilty.

"I'm getting tired of you spying."

"How else am I going to find out how to talk to boys or how to kiss boys? Why didn't you kiss him?" Trina stomped up the stairs.

"Why didn't I — ? Girls don't — " Lindsey started to call after her. Could girls take the initiative? she wondered. What if she'd kissed Bill, just a friendly kind of kiss? Would that have seemed too forward? Were there some things that never changed?

Her heart felt as if it had entered a race and was determined to win as she thought of the possibility. But she wasn't sure she had the nerve to find out what would happen if she did.

Twelve

"Bill's here!" Trina shouted excitedly. "Piper, stand still! Oh, Lindsey, catch him before he runs out the door and ruins his costume."

Lindsey caught Piper in the entry hall, clad in his royal blue shorts and matching T-shirt, and turned him over to Trina before opening the door.

"Good morning," Bill said. "You look great! And so does Piper!" He petted the dog, who squirmed to get loose from Trina's arms.

"Do you think he'll win?" Trina asked.

"I'm not a judge," Bill said. "He has a good chance." He turned back to Lindsey and whistled softly under his breath.

Lindsey was pleased that Bill noticed the outfit she'd spent hours putting together. She'd decided to dress for the booth, choosing her white pants and her pink cotton sweater with the tiny red and white heart design at the neck. Had he noticed the tiny red heart she'd drawn on her cheek just beneath her left eye? That had taken forever to get perfect.

"Let's go," Bill said. "We want to be there for the grand opening."

As she sat beside him in the station wagon and looked out at the spring green lawns, still damp with dew, and newly leafed trees, shaking their branches to the gentle morning breeze, Lindsey felt an excitement in the pit of her stomach. The whole world looked new, and that's how she felt — new and ready. She glanced at Bill. He looked back and smiled.

The gym was cool and empty. The smell of fresh paint lingered in the air. Lindsey felt as if she should tiptoe across the wood floor. Being there before all the noise and excitement started was a little like being in an empty theater before the people came and the show started. A sense of anticipation hung in the air; the ghosts of fun-to-come were everywhere. She walked over to the kissing booth. Would her idea be as successful as she hoped? She reached up to straighten her sign and crossed her fingers for luck.

"Step right up, ladies and gentlemen. See artistic wonders of every kind at our craft booths; sample the savory delights of our food booths; try your luck at our games. Win, win, win. And don't forget our shows to entertain you and a kiss for luck before you leave." Bill stood in the center of the floor on top of the school insignia and waved his arms like a barker. "Right this way, young lady. Dunk the principal? Enter your pet flea in our beauty contest — never have I seen such a beautiful flea."

"Where? Where?" Lindsey asked. "Oh there." She slapped her arm. "Oh, no! Crystabelle, I'm sorry."

"Psst." Bill lowered his voice and put his hand near his mouth. "I hear there's a place where you can get a free hug."

"Really?" Lindsey asked, lowering her voice, too.

"Mm-hmm." Bill nodded slowly.

"Where?" she whispered.

"Here." Suddenly Bill put his arms around her. His closeness made her pulse race. "Now we've practiced for your booth," he said letting her go. "Come on. Let's uncover the pool and turn the heater on. We don't want Mr. Harley to turn blue." He grabbed her hand and pulled her toward the door.

Lindsey was certain her feet hardly touched the floor as she followed him. The thought, What if we'd been giving out real kisses at the booth? flickered through her mind. She pushed it away. No sense in reading more into Bill's gesture than what it probably was — a hug of exuberance in anticipation of the day's events. They'd worked hard and carnival day had finally come. If only. . . .

By nine all the workers were there and the booths were open for business. By ten the beauty contest entrants were arriving.

Never had Lindsey seen such an assortment of animals. Dozens of pets, including parrots and parakeets, cats and dogs, a goat, and even a pony, were led onto the school grounds. One little boy brought his goldfish, and there were a number of insects, spiders, and snakes. John and his assistants directed the entrants toward the sign-up table where they could register their pets for consideration in a variety of categories: biggest pet, smallest pet, prettiest, ugliest, longest, shortest, tallest, most unusual, best costume, etc. Teachers and members of the PTA had volunteered to be judges.

Lindsey spotted Trina and Kelly with Piper. He wasn't being very cooperative. "Good luck," Lindsey called before moving on. She'd soon have to return to the gym and her turn at the kissing booth. Her group had arrived promptly and Tom had the schedule well organized.

Near the fence, cheers went up from the crowd as Mr. Harley mounted the dunk tank platform. A long line of ticket holders formed immediately. The principal wore Ryan's sleek black wetsuit. His bald head glistened in the bright spring sun. He waved and smiled as he eased himself onto the seat overhanging the pool.

Lindsey glanced at her watch. It was time. She hurried to her booth where she would be on duty for the next hour. She was pleased to see a long line waiting for kisses. She slipped behind the curtain marked "boys only."

When her first customer stepped into the booth, she laughed to see that it was Quincy from the Franklin Lumber Company. She handed him a small plastic bag filled with candy kisses.

"Oh, ho," he said. "Pretty tricky."

"No sweeter kisses anywhere," Lindsey said. "Please keep our secret."

"All right." He sounded disappointed.

"And for being a good sport, you get a hug."

"Now that was worth a buck," said Quincy. "I might get back in line." He winked at Lindsey and she laughed.

"Who was that?" Keith Goldman, the boy on duty with her, asked.

"The salesman from the lumber company. He said he would come to the carnival."

Keith shook his head, then turned his attention to Marilee Roth who'd stepped behind the curtain. She got her money's worth with the hug he gave her.

"I'm going to tell my friends to get in line for this booth," she said.

"Don't give away our secret," Keith reminded her.

"No way," said Marilee. "I love surprises like you, Keith."

Keith turned a becoming shade of pink.

"I'll be back," called Marilee.

Lindsey's first hour passed quickly. She took her break when Grace came to take her place.

Where was Bill working? Lindsey wondered, as she stepped into the throng that milled about the gym. The scent of hot dogs and popcorn made her realize that she hadn't eaten much for breakfast. After buying a variety of tickets having values ranging from twenty-five cents to a dollar, she went to the food booth to buy a hot dog and lemonade.

Blaine, wearing a Woodcreek cap and a blue apron, said that business was tremendous. "People are eating everything but the wrappers," she said. "I hope we don't run out."

"It would be the first time that has happened if you do. Have you seen Bill?" Lindsey dabbed mustard from the corner of her mouth.

"Not for a while. He's here somewhere. And listen, visit the magic show and the mimes if you have a chance. Alicia lined up some real talent. They're terrific!"

"I'll try." A family of four came to order hot dogs, so Lindsey stepped out of the way. "I'll see you later, Blaine," she said.

Feeling slightly claustrophobic from the press of the crowd, Lindsey stepped outside, where Ms. Devonshire, the theater arts teacher, was doing face painting. Lindsey wondered if the heart beneath her eye was still noticeable.

Nearby, the merry-go-round spun slowly.

The gleaming faces of the children made it obvious that this ride was a big hit again.

Shouts and laughter drew her toward the dunk tank again. Mr. Harley had been replaced. Lindsey gasped as she saw who now occupied the platform. Bill perched on the tenuous seat, swinging his legs, and daring the crowd to try to knock him into the water. "There's not a pitcher in the place," he taunted. "Couldn't hit the side of the school if you stood two feet from it."

Lindsey pushed her way closer. She had two fifty-cent tickets left in her pocket. She handed one to Monica, who was assisting, then waved to Bill. The look on his face as she picked up the first of three balls was priceless.

"Aw, she can't throw," Monica called. "You don't have to worry, Bill."

"That's right. I was only captain of the girls' softball team in junior high," Lindsey announced. "I'm probably rusty by now." She took a few warm-up swings without letting go of the ball. At Woodcreek, Ross had taken all of her time and she'd given up softball. It felt good to hold one again.

Bill covered his eyes and pretended to be afraid.

Lindsey was laughing so much she completely missed the target paddle that released the catch on the seat.

Bill wiped his brow and waved. "Look at Miss Lindsey," he called. "She can't even come close." He pulled up one leg and rested an elbow on his knee, trying to appear nonchalant.

Two more throws. Lindsey took her time. She concentrated. She wound up and threw. Blam! The second ball hit the target right on center.

"Aaah!" Bill shouted as the seat gave way and he fell into the pool.

The crowd cheered. "Way to go!"

"You showed him."

"Okay, Lindsey!"

Minutes later Bill climbed the ladder and was reseated. "Beginner's luck," he called.

"That must mean that I'm a pro now," she answered. "Hold your nose, Bill. I'm going to douse Stark the Spark." Before he could reply, the third ball sent him into the water again. The crowd cheered again and clapped.

"Had enough?" she asked.

"Wait until I visit your booth," he called.

What did he mean by that? Lindsey wondered. She waved and eased back into the crowd. Others stepped forward, eager to try their hands at unseating Bill once more.

Back in the gym, she spotted her parents and hurried to say hello. "Where's Trina?" she asked.

"She took Piper home. We have a prizewinning dog," her father said. He held out a box of popcorn to her and she took a handful.

"What did he win?" Lindsey asked.

"We promised Trina we'd let her tell you about it," her mother said. "Your father has said too much already."

"I won't let her know you let it slip, Dad," Lindsey said. "Are you having fun?"

"A great time," said her father. "This school carnival gets better every year."

"Thanks, Dad." Lindsey put her arm around him. "Don't forget the kissing booth."

"Oh, we've already been there," her mother said. "Very clever, dear."

"Dad helped. He donated the kisses," Lindsey said. "I have to go. I want to see what some of the crafts booths have for sale, then it's my turn to be on duty again. See you later. Oh, and don't miss the dunk tank. It's fun. Give it a try."

"We'll go there now," her mother said, and they turned toward the exit.

At the crafts booths, Lindsey bought a crocheted belt and a hand-painted heart pin with her initial on it. She made her way back to the kissing booth. After all their planning, the day seemed to be speeding by.

"Go have fun, Sherry," she said as she stepped behind the curtain. "Thanks for helping out."

"I've been having fun," Sherry said, "but I'm starting to feel a little scrunched, if you know what I mean."

"Yeah," Lindsey said. "Some of those guys give bear hugs back."

Sherry's red curls bounced as she nodded. "What did you buy?"

Lindsey showed her.

"Oh, that pin is darling! Where did you get it?"

"Second craft booth to the left of the drinking fountain."

"That's where I'm going first." Sherry was gone in a second.

As Lindsey gave out candy kisses and hugs for good sports, she was surprised at how nice everyone was about not getting a real kiss.

Then Ross Jordani stepped into the booth. "Hi, babe. I'm ready for my kiss." He put his arms around her possessively.

Forcing herself to remain calm, Lindsey eased out of his grasp. "Then here you are." She handed Ross a package of candy kisses.

He looked at the bag she put in his hand, then tossed it back into the box. "I didn't pay a dollar for any chocolate and chewy junk. I paid a dollar for a kiss, babe." He pulled her close and kissed her.

Lindsey didn't return his kiss. As his lips pressed against hers she felt nothing and thought of nothing. There weren't even sad memories at his touch.

"If you'd been a good sport, you'd have got a hug," Lindsey said as he let her go.

"Good sport! Big deal!" Ross's mouth curled with disdain. "Games. I play for keeps, babe."

"No you don't, Ross," Lindsey said calmly. "You don't play at all. And you lose."

As he pushed his way out of the booth, Lindsey wondered if she had ever really loved him at all.

Tom, who was beside her, grinned and

gave her an okay sign as the next girl stepped around the curtain. Lindsey forgot about Ross and stared at her sister Trina.

"I thought you'd be Bill Stark," she said, looking up at Tom.

"Well, you can get your kisses from me," Tom said. He handed her a bag of candy.

"These are the kisses? I should have brought Piper for these."

Lindsey laughed.

Trina frowned. "What are the hugs?"

Tom put his arms around Trina and hugged her. Trina's face turned pink, then red. "Oh," she said. "The hugs are nice. Maybe I'll get in line again."

Tom smiled.

"Piper won a prize, Lindsey." Trina pointed to a ribbon hanging from her belt. "Second place for the longest ears. Dewey Roberts' rabbit had longer ones." She sighed. "I hoped he'd get most beautiful or best costume. I entered him in those categories, too. But most beautiful went to Jackee Gordon's cat and best costume went to Denise Sydney, who dressed her white rat as a ballerina."

"I'm glad you won," Lindsey said.

"I didn't really. Piper did." Trina glanced up at Tom. "See you later," she said. "Bye, Lin."

"That's my sister, Tom."

"I sort of guessed that. I wouldn't mind waiting a couple years for her," he said. "She's cute."

"Yes, she is," Lindsey said, as her next customer arrived.

"Hey, who or what is Piper?" Tom asked between kisses and hugs.

"Piper is our basset hound," she said. "Aren't you glad Trina didn't buy him one of your kisses? Have you ever hugged a basset?" She laughed at the look on Tom's face.

He peered around the curtain. "Whew!" Your sister is in line again, but no sign of a dog."

Lindsey looked out, too. And so sign of Bill, either, she thought. But he'd said he'd come. Had he meant it?

Thirteen

The Spring Carnival was over. Now the clean-up crews went to work. The committee was part of this group, and although each was exhausted, they stuck by the booths in their charge, making sure that what had not been sold was properly packed away. Last, the booths would be disassembled and stored away for next year.

At the kissing booth, Lindsey counted the remaining bags of candy. Only thirteen left. Not bad considering that they'd started with two cartons full, she thought.

Lindsey was glad to be alone for a while. The carnival marked a new beginning for her and a definite end to her relationship with Ross.

Her feelings were in a tangle. She was elated by the success of the day, but there was also a tinge of disappointment mixed in. Bill had never come to the booth. Couldn't he have bought at least one ticket, out of curiosity if nothing else? Lindsey sighed as she turned away from the box and stood on tiptoe to take down one of the curtains.

Throughout the gym she could hear good-natured banter among the kids who were helping return the gym and school grounds to normal.

"Is this booth closed?"

Lindsey turned away from the curtain she was taking down on the boys' side of the booth.

The person who had poked his head around the other curtain looked familiar, except for his reddish curly hair and a black mustache. "Is this where kisses are for sale?" he asked.

"Yes, but —" Lindsey smiled. "Bill, I'd recognize you anywhere. And red hair does not go with a black mustache."

"I cannot fool zees smart woman," he said in a fake French accent. He stepped around the curtain, bowed, and kissed her hand before taking off the wig and mustache. His hair was still slightly damp from his afternoon stint at the dunk tank.

"Well, we did it. A great carnival! Was your booth a success?"

"Mm-hmm. Almost sold out."

"If you're all out of kisses, I'll give you a few instead," he said, taking her hand in his. "It's only fair after you visited the dunk tank, don't you think? An equal exchange?"

But the way the kissing booth works —" Lindsey began.

He slipped his arms around her. "My kisses are free. Do you mind?"

Lindsey's knees felt weak. She could only shake her head. She closed her eyes as his lips touched hers gently. He held her close when their kiss ended.

"Everything went perfectly," she murmured.

"Yes, it did. Everything." He seemed not to want to let her go. Finally he stepped back. "I have something for you."

Lindsey looked up at him. "What?"

"A dozen tickets." He pulled a handful of them from his pocket.

"Well, then you deserve at least a dozen more kisses," she said. Her heart was beating as if she'd run a marathon. Lindsey stepped past him and opened the box. "Here you go." She scooped up the last packages of candy and handed them to Bill. "A baker's dozen at that."

He laughed. "I love an independent girl," he said. "Now, where're my free hugs?" He put the candy aside and held out his arms.

Lindsey went into them, hugging him back; then she kissed him lightly. Taking the initiative is okay, she thought, when you know it's what he wants, too.

"Bill, what were you going to ask me that day by the duck pond?" She could hear his heart beat beneath her ear as she rested her head against his chest.

"The day by the duck pond. Let's see? That seems like years ago."

"Don't tease," she said. "I'm serious."

"Oh, yes. So was I. I was going to ask you if you thought we could be more than just friends."

"We can," she said, hugging him again. "Why didn't you ask me then?"

"I wasn't sure you were ready to answer. I thought maybe Ross was still in the picture."

"Ross isn't anywhere," she said, looking up at him.

Bill smiled, then their lips met in a more serious kiss this time — a kiss that said they'd be partners long after the carnival was over.

"A kissing booth was a great idea," Bill murmured.

"Mm-hm," Lindsey agreed as their lips met again.

"Hey, Lin." Blaine poked her head around the curtain. "Whoops! I didn't know this booth was still in business. I'll come back later."

Neither Bill nor Lindsey flinched. "Eight more kisses to go," he whispered as he held her tight.

Lindsey wrapped her arms around his neck and pulled him close. "Who's counting?" she whispered.